THE NAVIGATOR

BOOK ONE OF THE NAVIGATOR SERIES

CHEYENNE RICHARDS

CONTENTS

For Barbara LaTour

Who lived the truth that a woman may be both fierce and cherished.

PREFACE

In 1848, San Francisco had just eight hundred residents. Then gold changed everything.

Within a few years, more than a hundred thousand prospectors flooded her shores—so overwhelming her fledgling economy of goods and services that many were in danger of starving.

They needed food and liquor, bowls and boots, stoves and cart wheels. Their pockets burst with gold dust, but the stores were bare.

This did not go unnoticed in New York.

Shippers quickly realized that if they could get their goods to the world's hottest marketplace, they could sell a single egg for three dollars. A shovel for fifteen. A quart of spirits for forty. One voyage to California could yield more profit than years in any other trade.

But the distance was their enemy.

Decades before the Panama Canal and transcontinental railroad, it took a grueling six months to ship cargo from New York around Cape Horn to San Francisco—keeping miners from their goods and merchants from their profits.

So they built faster ships. Not plodding Clydesdales built for stowage, but racehorses designed for speed above all else. The clipper ship was born—a revolutionary hybrid of privateer and opium smuggler.

And the race was on.

The voyage dropped to five months. Then four. When Captain Waterman made it in a blistering 97 days, he was hailed as a hero on both coasts for a feat surely never to be beaten.

His fame lasted barely a year.

On August 31, 1851, the *Flying Cloud* dropped anchor in San Francisco Bay after a record-shattering voyage of just 89 days.

Stunned miners lined the hills to cheer her in. Newspapers from California to New York to Sydney trumpeted the "Extraordinary Passage." The *Flying Cloud* became an instant icon—inspiring books, paintings, songs, and brand extensions. To this day, her image graces Anchor Steam beer bottles, and an Airstream trailer bears her name.

Her captain, Josiah Perkins Creesy of Marblehead, Massachusetts, became one of the most legendary sailors of all time.

But what is far less known about this true story is a fact that seems almost more impossible than the record itself.

The *Flying Cloud*'s navigator—the one who charted the route, set the courses, and saved the ship from wrecking in a furious Cape Horn storm, where one miscalculation could have sent ship and crew to the bottom of the world's most treacherous waters—was a woman.

Her name was Eleanor Horton Prentiss Creesy, and the record she set with her husband would stand for 135 years.

But Ellen's journey didn't begin with that voyage—nor did it end there.

It began in quiet acts of courage and small rebellions. Long before she broke records or crossed oceans, she defied expectations simply by stepping aboard. In an era when women were expected to be silent and still, small and safe, she charted a course that was anything but.

And that's where this story begins—not with triumph, but with choice.

Before you sail with Ellen...

Three little surprises are waiting for you—part history, part mischief—all crafted to make the world you're about to enter that much more fun. (A tiny hint: 🌷 🍪 ☠️). Claim them in ten seconds:

cheyennerichards.com/navigatorgifts

PROLOGUE

January 1830

The *Californian*'s deck groaned beneath Ellen's feet like a living thing, sensing danger. One moment, the Cape Henlopen lighthouse had stood as a bright beacon against the gray horizon; the next, a blanket of fog had devoured the whole of sea and sky around her. The timing couldn't have been worse. All around them lay the jagged teeth of the Hen and Chickens Shoal.

Ellen's fingers trembled against the worn chart of Delaware Bay, clipped to the board she'd brought topside for the run into Lewes Harbor.

"Of course you can do this, Eleanor Prentiss," Captain Papa had said before he collapsed at the helm, fever burning through him like wildfire. His last raspy command before they'd carried him below: "Have Ellen set the course."

Five simple words had transformed her from the crew's lucky

charm—the captain's quirky daughter with her curious gift for navigation—into the person responsible for their very lives.

She was barely sixteen years old.

No longer one of Captain Papa's lessons, this was the moment she'd dreaded—and dreamed of—in equal measure.

The chance to prove that she was worth her salt.

But the responsibility of the task hung far heavier than she'd ever imagined. Eight souls, a hundred tons of dried cod, and an eighty-foot coastal schooner—hers to keep safe as they cut blindly through treacherous waters. She saw the crew's sidelong glances—questioning, doubtful—their discomfort as palpable as the damp air that clung to her cotton dress.

With a pencil stub, she marked her last three-bearing fix and frowned. They were far too deep into the hazards to stand off and await better conditions. They'd be more likely to wreck by turning around than by holding course.

But the shoals covered two-thirds of the bay's opening, and to reach the safety of the Sears, she'd need to make two precisely timed course changes. Both of them inside 'The Devil's Cauldron,' the area of deadly rips and swirling eddies that could spin a vessel like a child's top.

If she calculated wrong and they hit a shoal, they'd rip the keelson right out of the bottom of the boat and sink her in mere minutes.

Ellen shivered and wished for a coat, but it was too late to leave the deck. Blinded by the fog, she'd have to navigate the dangerous passage entirely by mathematics. To even guess their current position from moment to moment, she'd have to rely on evolving estimates of deduced reckoning—shortened as all sailing language was inevitably condensed, to dead reckoning.

This meant calculating the schooner's speed and direction against the current's speed and direction.

"Remember, Ellie," Captain Papa had said on the last run, "The Hen and Chickens don't play fair. If the ebb runs hard against an easterly, you'll face eight different streams in a quarter mile braiding themselves through those shoals."

"ALL HANDS!" Mr. Gannett bellowed, the first mate's voice carrying the authority Ellen knew hers lacked. "Reef the mainsail!"

The crew scrambled to grab the tarred hemp lines with calloused hands, their movements quick and precise despite the tense set of their shoulders.

Reefing was a practical choice—they had enough speed for steerage and if they were going to hit a shoal, they'd best do it slowly—but it deviled her calculations and robbed her of the men she needed to run the log and the lead.

Ellen closed her eyes, summoning the tables she'd created over the past two years—each page in her neat hand. Countless nights she'd stayed awake, measuring, recording, and memorizing data, while gritting her teeth at Mr. Gannett's endless jokes over her efforts.

"Ain't seen numbers sail a boat as yet, Miss Ellen."

But what he called her 'remarkable luck' at fixing their position was her certainty, distilled into figures and formulas.

Now, those same tables told her what would happen to their speed as they reduced sail, and how long it would take them to complete the maneuver. She ran the calculations in her head—no time to use the slate—and penciled a dashed line onto the chart to estimate where they'd be in a quarter hour.

If she'd estimated correctly, it would put them right at the mark for the first course change. If she was wrong, the first sign would be a thunderous crash.

THE FOG ENVELOPED THEM, swallowing the ship piece by piece. First the tops of the two masts, then the bowsprit, until Ellen could barely make out the helmsman ten feet away. The mist beaded her eyelashes. All external reference points—gone. Just like the lessons Papa gave her, blindfolded, making her navigate by feel and memory alone.

As soon as the crew finished reefing, Mr. Gannett surprised her by calling for a second maneuver. "Prepare to wear ship," he ordered.

Ellen gasped. On the chart, she traced her finger along a long stretch of shallows just to starboard, little more than fathom deep. The *Californian* needed two fathoms to clear the bottom. With the rocky shore to larboard, where did Gannett think he was going to find room to turn around?

She opened her mouth, then closed it.

Who was she to contradict a fifty-year-old man?

Yet Papa had been clear. *Have Ellen set the course.* If he found out later that she'd neglected her duties, she'd be in dreadful trouble. Worse, she realized, he'd probably never have the chance to find out, because they'd all be dead within minutes if she didn't speak up.

"Belay that, Mr. Gannett, and hold your course," she said, pitching her voice lower, closer toward Captain Papa's register. "We've depth enough yet."

The mate's weathered face hardened, creases deepening. His eyes narrowed as he stepped close enough that she could smell the tobacco on his breath.

"Begging your pardon, Miss Ellen," he said, voice low enough that only she and the helmsman could hear, "but we'd best put about." He glanced meaningfully toward the companionway where her father lay sick below. "No disrespect to the Captain's judgment . . . but this ain't no place for a child to be making decisions."

The words stung, sharp as the biting January air, but Ellen drew herself up, standing as tall as her five-foot frame allowed.

"We could have worn ship an hour ago, or on a flood tide, but we've not the sea room for it now. Our only chance is to see this through." She held his gaze, refusing to blink first. "You've sailed with my father for twenty-eight years. Have you ever known him to be wrong about a heading?"

"No, Miss." The words came grudging as rusty hinges.

"Then trust him now. Trust me."

The words hung suspended in the damp air, weighted with all the times Mr. Gannett had patted on the head for her "pretty little numbers." She watched the struggle in his expression—weighing the risk of a girl's calculations against disobeying his captain's direct order.

The crew around them stopped moving as the tension grew.

Her throat tightened. What if he didn't listen? Or did he know something she didn't? What if he was right and her calculations were wrong? These six men would never see their families again. Mama would lose a husband and daughter at the same time. And it would all be her fault.

The weight of command pressed down on her shoulders like a physical mass.

"We've come too far to turn tail," she said, loud enough for the crew's ears. "Hold course. Eyes on the lead. When we make it to Lewes Harbor, I'll buy every man here a drink."

A chuckle broke the crew's tension but the mate's jaw remained clenched, a muscle twitching beneath his leathery neck.

Ellen pressed her palm against the smooth wood of the binnacle, drawing strength from its solid reality, from the compass needle that danced and settled, danced and settled with the *Californian*'s gentle roll.

Numbers don't lie, she thought.

Gannett's eyes flicked to Mr. Caleb, the oldest hand aboard, whose white beard was stained yellow with tobacco, hands gnarled as knots. The grizzled sailor gave an almost imperceptible nod.

"Steady on," Gannett finally responded, "Aye."

Ellen released the breath she hadn't realized she was holding, careful not to let her relief show.

The knot in her stomach didn't ease—it couldn't yet—but something warm unfurled in her chest. The validation of being heard, however reluctantly.

In the unnatural silence, Ellen could hear the muffled creak of straining ropes, the flutter of canvas, the water rushing by the hull.

"On my mark, we'll come to a heading of nor-by-nor'east," she said to Mr. Gannett.

The First Mate stared into the thick cotton of fog, then sighed. "Prepare to tack," he ordered.

Ellen ran her calculations again and again, staring at the chart. They should be close to the bend in the safe path through the shoals now, but if she was either too soon or too late, it would spell disaster.

"Learn to see the invisible, El," Papa always said. "The sea keeps secrets from those who rely only on sight."

Ellen closed her eyes. Listening with her whole body, she heard a sound like the breath of a viper, three points off the larboard bow. The siren song of the Hen and Chickens: water breaking over rocks.

Just where she'd anticipated they'd be.

"Mark," she told Mr. Gannett, and he relayed her orders to the men.

The canvas flapped as the ship swung to its new heading, and Ellen steadied her stance as the deck canted in the opposite direction.

Her calculations were either perfect or fatally flawed. One error, and the *Californian* would join the splintered wrecks that littered the bay floor.

"Steady," she cautioned, hands suddenly clammy as she flipped the sand glass again to keep the time. "Lead the line."

Mr. Tillerman rushed to the rail as if glad to have something to do other than wait for his doom. Unwinding the marked rope with practiced motions, he swung the lead in wide arcs before releasing it into the sea.

"By the mark, six!" he called moments later, the line jerking in his hands.

Six fathoms. Thirty-six feet of water beneath their keel. Close to the shoal—dangerously close—but based on the soundings on the chart, precisely where Ellen had calculated they would be.

Her heart leapt, but a murmur rippled through the crew.

Too shallow for comfort. Too risky for a girl's judgment. She could read the doubt in the hunched shoulders, the tight lips, the quick exchanges of glances, in the way hands tightened on railings and ropes.

"Maintain course," she commanded, forcing certainty into her voice despite the flutter in her chest. "We're crossing the shoal's outer edge exactly as plotted."

THE NEXT COURSE change would have to be just as precise, but the currents danced even stranger as they edged toward the bay's opening, and her heart tensed, wanting confirmation. She could have read the current set on the water—if she could have seen more than a few feet of it.

Then she had an idea.

She unclipped her chart and stepped to the taffrail.

"Mr. Tillerman, would you mind throwing this overboard?" She said, handing him the navigation board. "Directly off the stern, if you please."

The man gaped. His face drew wrinkled into a confused scrunch, then softened as he puzzled out her intent. "Aye," he said. "Aye!"

He dropped it carefully, ensuring it hit the water flat, where it floated for several minutes before succumbing to the deep.

But several minutes was plenty for Ellen to watch carefully as it bent off to starboard, to measure the exact angle of the current's set. To confirm her calculations.

"Bring her to west-by-nor'west, Mr. Gannett," she said.

Once the maneuver was complete, she called again for the lead. For several agonizing minutes, the only sounds she heard were the creak of timber and the slap of waves against the hull. Ellen fought to keep her face composed, though her mind raced through tide tables, sounding charts, and the dozens of passages she'd observed from her father's side.

"By the deep, seven!"

Ellen's shoulders eased a fraction. Deeper water now. She was right. The *Californian* responded beneath her feet, moving more freely, as if the ship itself sighed with relief.

"By the deep, nine!"

They were through the worst of it. Mr. Tillerman shook his head in amazement. Mr. Patrick cast an appreciative glance her way.

"Nicely done, Miss Ellen," murmured Mr. Caleb as he passed.

The simple acknowledgment from the crusty old sailor meant more than a thousand compliments on a new dress.

An hour passed in the strange, muffled world of white as Ellen continued her careful dead reckoning. The chart, now laid on the binnacle, grew damp beneath her hands, but each mark brought a particular satisfaction that settled in her bones with a rightness that made her almost dizzy.

This feeling—this knowing—differed from anything she'd experienced in the parlors where she was expected to flourish.

Finally, as if granting mercy, the fog thinned, revealing patches of lead-colored sky, and the beam of the lighthouse breaking through.

"There!" Mr. Caleb shouted from the bow. "Lewes Harbor, dead ahead!"

A cheer rose from the crew, echoing across the water. The same men who'd looked at her with skepticism now nodded respectfully, their boots thudding against the deck with newfound vigor.

Something broke loose inside Ellen's chest—a wild, soaring feeling of triumph that threatened to burst from her like a physical force.

This—this—was who she was.

Every calculation confirmed, every correctly predicted fathom, was a vindication of her true self.

Her place wasn't in Marblehead as Mama would have it, paying calls and studying fashion magazines 'like a proper young lady.' Her place was here—guiding a vessel through unseeable dangers with nothing but her mind and mathematics to guide her.

Mr. Gannett approached, his posture a fraction more deferent. "Wouldn't have believed it possible," he said, "if I hadn't seen it myself. Your calculations were . . ." He trailed off, as if the words themselves rebelled against his tongue.

"Precise," Ellen said, savoring the word like a sweet cake on festival day. "Mathematics doesn't care if I wear skirts, Mr. Gannett."

BEFORE HE COULD RESPOND, a haggard figure appeared at the companionway. Captain Papa clutched the railing, his knuckles white with effort. His face was pale and damp with sweat, but his eyes were clear with pride as they found her—the same hazel as her own, holding the same determined set.

"El," he whispered hoarsely, the word carrying despite its softness.

She rushed to steady him. His body burned against hers, too hot, too frail, the once-powerful frame now trembling with the effort to stand. "Papa, you shouldn't be up."

He waved away her concern, scanning the harbor entrance now clearly visible before them—the familiar silhouette of warehouses and church steeples. He pulled the chart from her fingers and traced the pencil marks that told the story of their blind passage, lingering on each one.

"That's my navigator," he said, voice rough with fever but vibrant with pride. "Sharp as a compass and twice as reliable."

In that moment, Ellen Prentiss felt the certainty of her place in the world lock into position, as fixed and immutable as the stars.

She glanced at the harbor and no longer saw a destination, but a beginning. Her beginning.

Her fingers had always been clumsy with needle and thread, and her kitchen forays often ended in disaster, but for the first time in her life, she felt powerful. She was neither hopeless at girl things, nor a girl playing at boy things. She was a navigator, successfully doing navigator things.

She belonged at sea. This truth—like her carefully plotted sights—would never change.

She couldn't wait to get home and tell Perk the story. A real-life adventure at sea, just like they'd been dreaming about. And if she could do this, certainly she could calculate a way to rescue him from the drudgery of his father's ropewalk. He just needed a chance to get out of Marblehead and see what was possible.

She turned back to Captain Papa and caught something in his fever-bright eyes—a fleeting shadow of concern as he glanced at the crew. A chill that had nothing to do with the January air slithered down her spine.

But she pushed the thought away, focusing instead on the solid reality of Lewes Harbor, the tangible proof of her success.

Her calculations had been perfect.

Certainly, her future would be too.

1

———————

January **1841**

Of course you can do this, Eleanor Prentiss.

Ellen gritted her teeth and then forced a smile, determined to succeed in this as she had with every other challenge.

"What a lovely hat, Mrs. North."

The older woman spun around. Delight danced across her mouth —until she recognized the speaker.

"Thank you, Miss Prentiss." Her voice held the sharp edge of disappointment.

Ellen knew the dozen other people at Henry's oyster stand were listening intently, even as they pretended not to. Listening and judging.

Her dress. The contents of her market basket. Her being there at all. 'Oh how the high and mighty have fallen,' they must be thinking.

It would take time, Mama had reminded her. She wasn't hated, merely disliked. And she should be grateful for that much after twenty-six years of shunning polite society to chase salty adventures as if she thought herself a man.

But dislike she could come back from.

Ellen swallowed and tried again. "Such a pretty color of plum velvet. Does it come from Boston?"

Mrs. North glanced around, seeming to wrestle with whether to engage with the young lady who took after her father overmuch—a criticism Ellen had always felt as a compliment.

After a long sigh, Mrs. North seemed to settle on pity. "Your mother should teach you that a lady would call it a bonnet."

The heat rose in Ellen's cheeks. *Bonnet!* Of course she knew that. Had she really called it a hat? Thank goodness she'd not praised her sou'wester.

She heard Mama's voice in her head, reciting from *The Virtuous Wife* in a last ditch attempt to win Ellen a husband.

Be ever agreeable.

"I thank you for your valuable instruction, Mrs. North."

ACROSS THE SQUARE, a southerly wind spurred the skeleton elms into a somber dance before sweeping down the hillside, snapping Saturday market awnings, flogging neckties, and flattening the weary grass between the granite outcroppings.

As it approached the oyster stand, Ellen burrowed her face into her shoulder, but the gust discovered the thin gap between her wool skirt and button boots, burrowing straight through her pantalettes to give her legs an icy shock.

Still, she welcomed the pain, found that it fixed her inside her body again, into the world, after so many months adrift.

Precisely six.

The Marblehead Oil & Candle sign swung on its fastenings, creaking loudly. A solid Force Seven blow, Ellen calculated, pulling a milky blanket of cirrostratus clouds across the sun. When the wind shifted, it would do so with teeth.

The market day haggling turned to skyward glances as the fish-wives bundled their salt cod, and the daguerreotype man from New Bedford leaned over his specimens. But Ellen knew that while a hard nor'easter was on its way, the rippled wrack rode too high to carry rain today.

More's the pity.

"THE BONNET IS FROM LE HAVRE," Mrs. North said. "A gift from my son."

Ellen choked down a lump of jealousy, remembering how impatient she'd once been to reach her envisioned future, where she'd sail triumphantly into ports like Le Havre, Valparaíso, the Sandwich Islands, and everywhere else on the map. She'd never imagined her farthest voyage would end up being to Baltimore—nor that her actual future would trap her inside a land-based cage.

She tried to recall the name of Mrs. North's son but drew a blank. One of the boys that used to spit at her and Perk, though. She was sure of that much.

"Well, your son has wonderful taste."

Ellen wondered whether Mrs. North had attached the yellow silk pansy with her long-dead husband in mind. Pansy for remembrance. Yellow for a memory that brought comfort, not despair.

Ellen tried to turn another wave of envy into hope, but couldn't imagine ever being able to replace the stark white lily on her own mourning hat.

Bonnet.

Once last errand, though, and Ellen could return to the safety of the study. To the quiet of rolled charts, the warmth of lamplight, and the fading smell of his pipe tobacco. She could settle into his worn leather chair and watch the moods of the sea from the window, measuring the relative positions of Eastern Point and Baker's Light until her mind filled with nothing but angles and sines and cosines.

MAMA HAD BEEN RIGHT ABOUT one thing. The body remembers.

While Ellen still felt disassociated from everything outside the house after six months of isolation, her feet had found the steps to the market without trouble. Her mouth had formed words.

Each startling familiarity had brought a small astonishment. The cobbles still began at State Street. Mrs. Gannon still kept her daily vigil on the roof—same black shawl, same stare at the horizon, as if looking hard enough might conjure back her husband and son. Market Square was still wedged against the hillside, and shoppers still carried on as if nothing had irrevocably changed.

At least until they saw Ellen.

What Mama hadn't warned her was that each pitying glance, each well-intentioned sigh, would eat away her fortitude until she felt as fragile as Murano glass all over again.

She caught herself replaying the sequence of events for the millionth time, trying to change the outcome. If Mama hadn't taken ill. If Ellen hadn't stayed home to care for Mathilda. If she'd been on that last voyage to the Carolinas . . .

A FUZZY SHADOW moved across the ground, drawing her attention from her grief. It weaved between the thicket of boots and skirts until it paused beside Ellen's black wool coat. On closer examination, the form proved to be a curious Newfoundland pup exploring the mud, testing the slick ooze with each oversized paw as if surprised by how it stuck.

Mama had tried to interest her in town gossip, and she remembered some tidbit that included Henry the Goat's new dog. What had Mama called him? The adorable creature at her feet was lamp black but for a white cross on his forehead, small enough Ellen could have tucked him right in her basket between the crookneck squash and skein of yarn.

Fluke. That was it.

He fixed her with a playful look, bright-pink tongue hanging so merrily Ellen almost managed a smile.

It would have been her first in six months.

She felt a quiver of her spirit renew. A seed buried deep, just beginning to stretch under the ice, waiting for the thaw to send up fragile buds.

But the thought of spring flowers reminded her too quickly of the forget-me-not carefully pressed into the book by her bed, and she bit the inside of her cheek. That was a different memory. Ten years on, and still not nearly ready for a yellow pansy.

"—I'll be late, Father. You'll have to finish this yourself—"

That mockingbird voice.

Ellen made the mistake of looking up. Euphemia Bartlett had weaseled in front of her in line, wearing a peacock-blue silk dress—strangely coatless despite the frosty air. Next to her stood the lanky figure of the pastor. Why in heaven's name was he out doing the market shopping instead of his wife?

Ellen re-tucked her chin but wasn't quick enough to avoid Henry's observant eye.

"Miss Prentiss! Is that you?" His voice boomed from behind his table, causing every head to turn.

Oh God, Henry. Not now.

"So glad to see you out. I was so awfully sorry to hear about Captain Prentiss."

Ellen managed a weak nod and trained her eyes back to the ground, feebly trying to hide.

"Why, what a timely surprise." Euphemia's claws grabbed Ellen's arm. "We've missed you so at church, dear."

As always, bald-faced lies came as naturally to her as breathing.

Ellen drew her arm away, but braved a direct glance at Euphemia's pitch-colored eyes, at the grin that slithered across her face.

"The great lady navigator has finally set down her charts and joined us common folk on market day."

Euphemia's arrows had always been ruthless, but this one was also well-aimed. Ellen cringed at how many times she'd scoffed at Mama for asking her to help with the sweeping or baking or church socials, preferring to retreat into her maps and calculations instead.

"I'm honored to be doing such important work," Ellen said.

"I must say, it's brave of you to venture out today," Euphemia said. "You've heard the news then?"

Learn there is sometimes an adaptedness in silence, which gives a charm to conversation.

Ellen forced herself to maintain control of her expression, clutching the wicker-basket handle until the fibers groaned as she waited for an explanation. Then waited longer. As more heads turned, she knew she was merely being stubborn. There was only one way out of this squall, and that was through it.

"What news is that, Miss Bartlett?"

A surprised blink, then Euphemia's grin stretched halfway to New Bedford. "Why, today's arrival," she said, baiting.

Euphemia's skin had turned an angry pink in the cold, despite all the whitening creams, even as her face remained a perfect rock.

"Oh?" Ellen wondered if they were still children, trading petty jealousies. She grew bored and congratulated herself for not getting riled up. It seemed a good sign, like a tide pool refilling after an ebb.

Euphemia pursed her conniving mouth for what seemed like a full minute. "Well then. Go on, guess," she said, giving no quarter to the hollow ache of grief.

"Goodness," Ellen finally said. "Is it the ribbon maker up from Boston again?"

"Not even close," Euphemia answered.

"A music teacher from Providence?"

"You really don't know, do you?"

She seemed genuinely surprised and Ellen glimpsed what might almost have been pity as Euphemia's eye twitched in the cold.

"I can't be late," was all she said, though. And, "You'll find out soon enough."

She turned away with enough drama to spin her skirts into a peacock-blue eddy, then strode down the hill.

But not before three more words sliced through the air.

"If you dare."

The echo of the old taunt most certainly intended: *How dare you?*

Ellen had forgotten how menacing laughter could sound. She cursed herself for wondering, despite her every resolve, what had caused Euphemia to dress in her finest silks in the middle of January.

When she finally looked down, Fluke's curious nose had drawn him to the Bartlett's basket on the ground, and Ellen soon spied the reason for his interest. A thick lamb shank lay exposed among the turnips and salt cod. A strategic error that Mrs. Bartlett would never have made.

She watched the dog's careful approach, and this time she did crack a smile.

Get it, Fluke.

"One pottle or two, Miss Prentiss? I still owe you from the summer, you know."

It was as if Henry knew her worn reticule was down to just a picayune and two pennies. She was sure he meant well, peering at her over the crowd, but she felt the pity in her old friend's fictional credit, and his kindness burned.

SHE'D ALWAYS EMPHATICALLY BELIEVED she'd be the one woman in Marblehead to lead an independent life. She'd studied diligently, built sought-after skills, and earned what she'd imagined would be a lifelong position: navigator of the *Californian*.

But the past six months had taught her just how much her achievements had owed to Captain Papa's open mind as well. She sent a hundred and eighty-six letters, offering her services to every shipping company on the eastern seaboard. A few replies had been polite. Most had been curt. All had been clear. The only woman allowed on one of their boats—and even this to be generally discouraged—was a captain's wife.

Or a captain's daughter, she'd thought, ruefully.

Now, as she emerged from half-mourning, for the first time in her life, Ellen was trying to attract a husband.

There was no other way.

Discard from your speech all that bitterness which springs from disappointment.

"ONE'S PLENTY, Mr. Doyle—but I'll gladly wait my turn," she said.

"So, then . . ." Henry said, giving her a wink.

The crowd stared as Ellen fumbled, unsure in the silence. "I'm well enough, thanks," she said. "And you? Is little Hannah's cough better? I take it Mrs. Doyle's entirely recovered?"

Another gust caught Ellen's hair, yanking a stubborn dark strand free of her bonnet. She tucked it back with familiar annoyance—the same battle she'd fought since she was a girl and Mama declared her untamable locks a trial sent from above.

"No. Yes, I mean they're both fine, but tell me—what do you think?" Henry's eyes held a mischievous sparkle she couldn't fathom.

When she didn't answer, he thumped each oyster on the table, satisfied only when it sounded solid as a stone, then made change for Mrs. North.

What did Ellen think of what?

She could only guess he meant the new ferry. A paddle-wheel steamer had replaced the sleek old periauger on the run to and from New York. Progress, apparently, entailed a virgin sky smeared with coal smoke and brutish vessels that didn't glide through the sea so much as chop it to bits.

"Something of a stinkpot, I daresay."

The oysters that Henry was holding clattered to the table, and he squinted with incomprehension.

Oh, Ellen.

Adapt yourself to the prejudices of those with whom you converse, and enter their trains of thought.

"Why, Mr. Doyle. Don't mind me. I'm far more interested in your thoughts of the steamer."

Henry burst out laughing. "No, you goose. I mean—"

"—Oh!" the schoolmaster's wife said. "Oh, my!" She pointed, and all eyes turned to the ground.

Ellen had forgotten about Fluke. Fluke had not forgotten about the lamb. He was eight feet away, dragging the heavy shank backward through the mud.

Henry chuckled. The schoolmaster's wife laughed. Pastor Bartlett clenched his fists. Three long strides closed the gap, and then the yelp rang in Ellen's ears before she could even process the swift kick.

"What's wrong with you? He's just a puppy!" The words burst out before Ellen could stop them.

She rushed over and gathered the pup in her arms, succeeding in slathering her coat in muddy smears. He was trembling, but she cooed to him like an infant and he eventually relaxed in her grasp. Nothing broken, at least.

But when she turned back to the crowd, the market had fallen silent as the grave. Not a word of haggle. Not the clink of a coin.

The uncontrollable Ellen Prentiss had just spoken out against the pastor himself.

Surely, the end times had arrived.

Ellen understood the scale of her mistake immediately. The heat rose in her face as she handed Fluke to Henry. For all her efforts to reform her behavior, she'd been worse than disagreeable. She'd been opinionated. Obstinate. Disobedient, even. In public.

Even if she'd not accidentally thrown down such a challenge, the pastor would never have overlooked such a prime opportunity to take down the willful girl he'd fought tooth and nail since she could talk. She braced for the fiery, extemporized sermon that would soon outline for the whole market the litany of rules that God Himself had established, and the improper, hoyden, bluestocking Ellen Prentiss had broken yet again.

Those were some of the names he'd called her in the past, but now, without Captain Papa's protection, he might go as far as brazen hussy. Maybe even dangerous Influence. Any one of them would destroy her fragile hope of securing a husband in Marblehead for good. Maybe all of Essex County. With a few words he would ruin Ellen as surely as he had Abigail, Rebecca, and the tragic Mrs. Reed.

Bartlett secured his dinner and gathered his frown.

Ellen fought the urge to run. Fought it hard.

"I hope you consider yourself quite fortunate, Miss Prentiss," Bartlett said to her under his breath. "That I am in no humor to quarrel."

As her jaw dropped, he spoke louder, for the benefit of the crowd.

"During this unique and highly special time, I'm afraid all my attention has been drawn to the Lord's blessings and I've not heard you properly, Miss Prentiss. But I'm certain you must have conveyed your best wishes for Euphemia's wedding tomorrow. Is that right?"

Ellen still stood on defiant feet, braced for a boarding wave that never came. She nodded, woodenly, wondering if this was a trick. If he merely meant to prolong her suffering.

Then the substance of his words reached her.

Euphemia was getting married? To whom?

"The Bartletts thank you for your kindness," he continued, "And we look forward to having you join us in church tomorrow." He looked up at the crowd. "In fact, I'm sure you'll all be pleased to learn that because of certain . . . schedules, the wedding will replace our regular Sunday sermon."

Pastor Bartlett chuckled at his own uncharacteristic humility. Others laughed nervously.

Ellen backed away.

She was grateful for his mercy today, but still her hands shook. For how much longer could she fight her nature?

The fragile bonds holding her grief at bay suddenly snapped, and desperate loneliness rose in her with the violence of a typhoon.

The oysters were forgotten.

Step. Step. Watch the mud. Step.

She inhaled the loamy smell of the boot-churned earth—the next best thing to sea air. Found herself in front of the printer's shop. Rounded the corner at the Fountain Inn. Slipped. Caught herself. Scrambled forward. State Street. Lee Street. Front Street.

She was grateful the fish packers, shoe factories, and ropewalk were closed. No one behind those windows to watch her reach the cobbles and break into a run.

———

It wasn't until she reached the harbor that she realized her feet had known exactly where to take her. At Appleton's Wharf, she could attempt to renew her broken spirit with the warm haze of memory.

Her beloved schooner wasn't there, of course, but she could stand on that comfortingly solid quay, rest on the river stones worn smooth as slate, and in the quiet of a Saturday, still hear the echo of boot heels, the creak of pulleys, the synchronized harmony of a shanty. She could remember the cheekily upturned bowsprit and two proudly raked masts. The spot on the taffrail where Captain Papa cleaned his pipe.

She could rest for a while—if not quite in the past, neither fully in the present. Here, she could remember who she was. Not this unmoored buoy, bobbing uselessly in the shallows. Not this fragile vessel of a woman, the object of their pity and their scorn.

She was the fierce daughter of Captain Papa.

Accomplished mathematician.

Navigator of the *Californian.*

And also a woman who no longer had a father, a boat, or anything left to calculate.

WHEN VOICES INTERRUPTED HER THOUGHTS, she nearly let a sailor's curse escape under her breath.

She'd forgotten the ferry. Saturday it arrived from New York.

A small crowd was arriving just across the way at Parrock's Landing, to meet the steamer as it rounded the Neck—angry, frothing paddles closing fast.

She'd have no more memories today, no moment of peace. Would have to—

There was a peacock-blue dress among the welcome party.

Euphemia's great surprise must be coming from New York to see her wedding.

No, Ellen realized. Euphemia would never have risked her death of a cold for anyone but her groom. A wealthy cousin, probably. The Bartletts were a proud family. It would have to be someone of note. Not that Ellen cared.

Except, why did Euphemia think she would?

Curiosity got the better of her and she stepped behind the donkey cart, near the wall of the freight office, to remain out of view as the steamer drew closer.

Euphemia stood with a small group of people. Ellen was too far away to recognize them from behind. An older woman. A white-haired man with crossed arms. A young woman in a slate-gray coat—

That was Patience Creesy.

Her heart thudded in her chest even before her mind caught up.

Now that she knew what to look for, she could see instantly that the older woman was Mrs. Creesy. And that must mean—yes—that was Mr. Creesy as well.

If you dare, Euphemia had taunted.

But—

No. That was impossible.

THE STEAMER APPROACHED the landing at a rakish angle, requiring the boat hand to leap for his life to secure a line around the bollard. Ellen inched back into the shadows even as she scanned the rows of passengers at the rail.

No. No. No.

No. Certainly not. No.

Tall man. Broad as an elephant. Dark curls framing his face under a captain's hat. The same curls that used to fall across his eyes as they ran.

Good Lord.

It couldn't be.

Her legs trembled. She had to press her back against the warehouse wall. The taste of copper flooded her mouth.

Perkins Creesy.

A shadow over his face. No—it was a beard. When did that happen? How long had he been gone?

Ten years. Four months. Eight days.

Forever.

The memories hit her as a breaking wave. Perk climbing trees, that goofy laugh echoing across the bay. Perk playing war with sticks. Perk in the dory, trailing his fingers in the water. Perk handing her the forget-me-not.

Her stomach twisted into knots.

Perk not saying goodbye.

He wore a captain's hat, though. He'd done it, then. Hadn't she told him he would? A swell of pride blocked her throat.

The one person left on earth who understood who she truly was.

Could she could summon the courage to approach the quay? If she did, would he give her that wry half-grin of his or would he spit at her feet?

She steeled herself with guilt, if not hope. At least she could finally apologize. She owed him that much, and maybe—

Euphemia's wedding, she remembered. She was here to meet her groom on the steamer.

Perk was—

The stab of pain ripped Ellen nearly in half.

He hadn't been too busy to write for ten years. He'd been writing to someone all along—it just wasn't Ellen.

Perk had already spit at her feet.

The town's dislike she might one day overcome, but not Perk's hatred. Not ever.

It might have hurt less if she hadn't deserved every bit of it.

Fearless enough in the storm as they'd sailed from Salem, she'd turned coward as soon as they'd reached the beach. So sure she'd lose everything if she admitted the truth. Instead, it was her lie that had ruined everything.

Now, Perk had become a captain.

Euphemia, after all these years, would soon marry her secret crush.

Ellen was hiding behind a donkey cart in a mud-smeared coat, wild hair twisting in every direction, unable to even complete the market shopping. She'd lost her father, ship, income, identity, and pride. And reminded of her deepest shame, she now wondered if she didn't deserve all those losses.

Ellen took two steps back, then two more. Then stumbled over a root and fell to the ground.

What had become of her basket?

She edged around the buildings until she was back on Front Street, where she could make her way home unseen. A tightness gripped her belly. Snaked up her neck.

She'd won most of their childhood games, but he'd won the grown-up prize.

Ellen was elated for his success. Also, thunderstruck with self-pity.

When she finally reached her gate, she sliced her hand open, trying to force the latch. Inside, she didn't stop the front door from slamming. Didn't stop to hear which shanty Mathilda was singing to her doll. Didn't pause for Mama's lecture about "—gone all morning, eggs to be gathered, boots to be shined—"

She heard only the echo of her feet thudding on the risers, the click of the thumb latch into the study.

The floor swayed beneath her like a tilting deck.

Odd for it to do so on land.

She reached for the monkey rail to steady herself against the pitch and yaw, only to find there was no rail. There was no bulwark. There was only a table. A lamp. A dusty book hiding a pressed blue flower. There was only air.

And then the floor.

2

———————

Whatever was about to happen, Perk told himself he'd survived two days of worse.

He hefted his seabag, then fell in behind the other passengers at the rail, watching Marblehead heave into view.

He felt the heaviness of the air. The birds flying low over the water. A hard nor'easter would hit by Tuesday, complicating the *Oneida*'s departure from New York.

But that was too far out to plan. He had the weekend to survive first.

Letters chased sailors across oceans like gulls after fish scraps, often years behind, but the one Perk picked up at Grinnell's office in New York hadn't come from either Mother or Patience. It had taken him more than a minute to recognize his father's handwriting after so many years.

"Be glad of seeing you," Father had written. A note succinct enough to be cryptic.

.   .   .

For almost two weeks he'd tried to ignore the letter, to put his head down and take the tongue-lashing from Grinnell for being so late to market that the tea he brought had to be sold at cut rates.

Each day, he'd resolved not to take Father's bait. He'd been wary enough to avoid Marblehead for ten years and saw no need to alter course now.

Yet each night, lying awake in his bunk, he'd change his mind. Was there trouble? Could Mother be ill—or worse? The most disturbing question was whether his reticence to go home was practical or represented a streak of cowardice remaining in him.

Finally, when it was nearly too late, he'd cursed the blue devils and bought a ferry ticket. Then run around town buying gifts like a lunatic. Not from the Pearl Street hucksters, either, but the real things from Stewart's on Broadway. Two porcelain teacups, a lacquer box, and a jade necklace—at prices five times what they would have cost him in Canton.

Finally, he'd asked Grinnell for every cent remaining on his account. If there was trouble with Father, likely it would take Spanish dollars to solve.

As the steamer rounded The Neck, Perk found Marblehead both shockingly familiar and surprisingly different.

In the crescent-shaped harbor, the fishing schooners still rocked gently on their moorings. He took in their beamy black hulls and pinched sterns, each representing not only a family but a fishing ground, passed down for generations.

But where the harbor of his memory had felt as massive as the sea itself, after crossing oceans, he now saw nothing more than a pewter-tinted pond. Barely a cable's length across. A mere three fathoms deep. Had he really ever been that young? That naïve?

He was happy to see that the row houses were still built right up to the sand, still topped with widows' walks. The shore was also dotted as ever with the same brightly painted dories of his past, practically calling out to be let off their leashes.

Perk scanned them on the sand—green hull with white trim, green hull with red interior, gray hull with blue gunwales. Blue hull with yellow gunwales and a star at the bow. Old Man Doyle's boat.

He forced down one memory in that dory with a grimace, and focused instead on his first experience aboard: the beginning of his love for the sea.

Henry the Goat had taken Perk out in the Doyle boat when they were both ten. They'd rowed that open fifteen-footer out to the center of the harbor, stowed the oars, added the spritsail, and let the wind do all the work.

It had been a revelation.

Invisible power, harnessed. Captured. Directed at will.

So little he'd known about watercraft back then. Nothing but the ropes that held them. Now his practiced eye saw the vessels in front of him were built with flatter bottoms than the Gloucester boats. More stable thwarts than Swampscotts.

Pride filled Perk's chest before he noticed it coming.

Marblehead not only built the finest dories, it built the finest sailors. The best navigators. Everyone knew that. Salem could keep its deeper harbors and fancier manners, Boston, its grander State House and learned societies, New York, its wealthier shipyards and counting houses.

Marblehead had the better men. Fiercely independent. Practical. Straightforward.

It was Marblehead privateers the Brits had been most afraid of during the revolution. Marblehead sailors who'd formed the backbone of Washington's navy. Marblehead oarsmen who'd rowed his army across the Delaware.

For ten years, Perk had forced himself to think only of the next bell. The next day. The next leg. Avoiding everything that stunk of the past. But in coming home, Perk could finally see just how high he'd climbed from that beaten-down, lovesick, sixteen-year-old green-horn he'd once been.

Father could be damned for all he'd scoffed at Perk's seafaring dreams. He certainly couldn't ignore the results now. His son commanded a tea trader. One of the youngest captains in the fleet. The man would never praise, and certainly wouldn't apologize, but maybe Perk's achievements would warrant at least a slap on the back.

That alone would make the ferry trip worth the sleepless night trying to ignore the boiler's endless chuffing, the vibration that kept trying to shake his bones apart, and the stink from the furnace.

THE STEAMER THRASHED through the last half mile to Parrock's Landing. Was Father watching him? Mother? He swallowed a sudden fear that she'd passed. Father would have said so, wouldn't he?

The familiar odors of tar, brine, and rotting seaweed hit Perk the same as every other harbor from Liverpool to Canton, but this time with the unmistakable Marblehead additions of dead cod and caustic lime.

He scanned the small crowd, biting back the impulse to follow every flash of dark hair.

Thank God, Mother was the first he spotted, though only by her stately posture.

When had her hair turned gray?

At her arm was a young woman he barely recognized as Patience. She'd been nine when he left. Now nineteen.

Next to her, Father. Bareheaded in the bite of winter. Arms locked across his chest like a fortress wall. Smaller than the giant of Perk's memories, though.

One quick move and Perk could lift him clear off his feet if need be. He'd been a son of a bitch once, but that was before Perk had learned to strike a blow, avoid a knife, disarm a pistol in the cold, wet, dark—moves as natural now as breathing.

What threat was one old man next to all that?

Father sat at a desk. Shuffled papers. Bitched about taxes. Cut Mother down while her careful columns of numbers kept his business afloat time and again.

He'd let the old man speak first. Get the lay of the land. Stand stock still—

Mother's wave caught him off guard. His hand lifted before he could stop it, hanging there like a loose halyard. He swallowed the lump in his throat.

The gulls still wheeled, but the wharves had shrunk. Parrock's Landing had seemed so enormous when El—

No.

Perk grimaced. Brought his hand back to the rail. Gripped it hard enough to snap.

Father was enough to face. That girl was nothing but a ghost to him now.

THE DECKHAND PLACED THE GANGWAY, the other passengers scattered, and Perk tried to settle his face into a neutral greeting as he stepped onto the landing. Mother was beaming, though, and her face drew the grin right out of him.

She hauled him close, and he found himself wrapped in her arms. A full embrace.

He'd entirely forgotten such affection, and the feeling knocked him off-balance. The smell of Mother's lavender soap filled his lungs, and the memories flooded back. Watching her work at the washtub. The wet slap of clothing keeping time as she spun her tales. How Father's shirt had wrestled an octopus in the harbor. The runaway socks that joined the circus. The pillowcase that held the dreams of a sleeping giant.

The memories had him reeling.

Was he the captain who'd weathered typhoons, or the boy who'd hidden behind her skirts?

Patience clung to his side like a barnacle, her face pressed into his shoulder.

"I've missed ye both—" The words escaped before he could clamp down on them. Thank God he blinked back the sting in his eyes.

"—so glad to see you home safe, son—" Mother was saying.

"—barely recognize you—" Patience's voice held the tone of awe he realized he'd been secretly hoping to find by coming home.

He sank into their embrace, muscles going slack as Mother's forehead pressed against his temple and Patience squeezed his ribs.

For a decade, he'd been worked to the bone. Frozen. Poked. Slapped. Punched for mirth and malice. Drenched. Scalded. Cracked on the head with belaying pins. He'd felt the bite of challenge plenty, and the surge of triumph occasionally. He'd known respect, lately, in the way men straightened their spines when he passed. A few times, even felt the soft press of a woman's flesh.

But this—

This was different. This was love. Boundless as the deep.

His body had forgotten its weight.

He forced down the lump in his throat and peeled himself free before losing himself entirely. "Let's have a look at ye," he said. A survival tactic.

He traced the worry lines that had become etched on Mother's forehead, then the wet gleam in Patience's eyes. She'd grown taller than Mother, nearly reaching his chin now. And her middle had thickened—

His tongue fell dead in his mouth. "Is that—"

Her cheeks bloomed pink above her grin. "It is indeed, brother," she said. "Your niece or nephew will join us this spring."

Little Patience. All his memories of her included skinned knees and sneaking extra feed to the chickens. He cursed the oceans that swallowed letters whole.

"You remember Daniel Pierce?" Mother said. "The boot maker's boy. They were married last summer."

"Wonderful." He sounded more wooden than he intended, tried desperately to regain his balance. "Congratulations, Little P. Truly."

A flash of blue dress caught his eye, and his gut clenched. But no. Wrong girl.

It took that long for Perk to realize Father hadn't said a word.

He'd hefted Perk's seabag, though. That was different. Maybe he was extending an olive branch. Perk had to repeat his thanks twice to Father's good ear before he got a curt nod in return.

The woman in the blue dress stood next to Father, her skirt as beamy as a Thames coal barge. Her brittle smile tugged at his memory. Familiar face. Not unattractive. Not pleasant, either. Why was she there? And what in heaven's name was she doing out without a coat in January?

Mother's voice cut through the awkwardness. "Perkins, you remember Miss Bartlett, of course."

His arm shot out on instinct, muscles performing courtesies his mind had forgotten. "Miss Bartlett." His voice stiffened into the formal cadence he used with merchants and diplomats. "How nice to see you."

Both her hands wrapped around his, as suffocating as they were delicate. Euphemia, he remembered, working his hand free.

"It was your father's idea to invite Miss Bartlett along," Mother said, jaw set tight as a monkey's fist. When Perk found her eyes, the pointed glare she flashed him—their old warning when Father was in a black mood—made it clear she disagreed with the choice.

"What a surprise," Perk forced out through gritted teeth. "Aye. Pleasant. Indeed." He clamped his jaw shut, or else he would have stammered his way into next week.

Father strode toward the house, leaving Perk little choice but to follow.

The old wharf timbers groaned with the cold. Father might've been pushing fifty or more, but he still moved like a wharf rat, forcing Perk to match his pace as he hit the cobblestones.

Perk tried to avoid looking south, but he couldn't help a glimpse between the salt houses at the ropewalk. That unmistakable structure, longer than a city block and barely wide enough to shelter a cart.

The barn-red paint had weathered away to naked planks, and visible holes said the roof needed major repairs, but his throat still tightened with memories. The building had been the bane of Perk's existence since he was seven and Father first belted the iron hooks to his waist, loaded them with hemp fibers, and commanded him to run backward along the covered ditch.

From that day till he was sixteen, dawn to dusk, Perk's legs had known nothing but retreat, choking on the fiber dust, palms bleeding, shoulders screaming, feeding strands out as Father spun at the wheel at the far end to twist them into rope. The binding forces were brutal. Yarns into strands, strands into hawsers, hawsers into cables—each twist adding tension, each rotation storing more power to snap back with deadly force if something broke.

One moment of carelessness, and those spinning ropes had once taken a man's arm clean off.

"Tell me of China, Perk." Patience bumped his elbow, eager, curious. Before he could plant his feet proper, she fired more questions. "If they eat with sticks, how do they manage soup? And is it truly the men who wear their hair in braids, rather than the women?"

"Dear," Euphemia broke in. "A virtuous woman encourages others to speak first."

Patience's shoulders tightened. Her steps grew stiff.

"One braid," Perk answered, grabbing Patience's arm and pulling her away from the sanctimonious blue cow. "It's called a queue."

The street seemed both familiar and warped now, like the twisting lanes had shrunk. "They eat well with their sticks, but they use a sort of spoon for soup. It looks a mite like a skiff with a handle."

The snow-covered roofs were lined with icicle teeth. The

wooden sign for Marblehead Oil & Candle creaked as it swung in the wind.

He'd beat Ellen—five rocks to two—at hitting it from the corner before Old One Eye had come out, mad as a hornet, and they'd made a run for it.

He suppressed a grin, but it only took the one lapse for memories to ambush him from every corner. Ellen beating him at chess. Ellen acting as lookout while he climbed Mr. Johnson's apple tree. Ellen making the treasure map to their secret cave by Outer Point Rock. Ellen's lie that poisoned them all.

"Are you alright, brother?" Patience asked. "Or is it your intention to break my arm in two?"

Perk loosened his grip on her elbow and tried to laugh his mood away, but the darkness of spite had returned.

———

Too soon, they arrived at the house. He recalled it being painted a stormy blue, but now only peeling flecks of color clung to the windowsill like snow and there was a visible sag to the roofline. The knots grew in his belly. The ropewalk hadn't been the only thing left to decay.

He was glad he'd brought the money for Mother. It was clear she needed it, and he cursed himself for not visiting sooner to see to her welfare.

All this time, he'd pictured their lives fixed in place, but change had crept in, quiet as a neap tide. Even the front door had shrunk. He had to fold his head down to clear the lintel.

The smell of fresh bread hit him full in the face, and he glimpsed the crisp linen napkins, precisely placed around five plates. Mother had set a place for Euphemia.

Perk's cap found its way to his hands, and he held it there, feeling the familiar worn brim between his fingers.

Patience crossed to the hearth, her skirts dusting the floorboards as she prodded the fire. "I've read they paint eyes on their ships in China."

Euphemia squeezed in behind him. "Where on earth would you read something like that?" she asked.

"Aye," Perk said. "One eye, each side of the bow."

He could have said more, but the room felt closer than he remembered. Tight with bodies. Father carelessly heaved his bag into the corner and Perk cringed, praying the straw would cushion the teacups.

He attempted to stand as tall as he did aboard, defiantly commanding two dozen men, but hit his head immediately on the beams. The old room forced his body into its old frame—shoulders hunched, spine curled. So he sunk into the nearest chair, instead.

Mother pressed a warm mug into Perk's calloused hands, the steam carrying the bite of cinnamon and sweet tang of apple that brought a smile—until she fixed him with a serious look.

"What he's about to ask of you," she hissed in her warning voice, "you must refuse."

The familiar register of her lowered voice, below Father's hearing, struck Perk.

"Is it money?" Perk whispered back. "I've brought—"

But Mother was shaking her head. "Keep your money. There is a plan. Trust me."

Now Perk knew he was in trouble.

"Euphemia's healthy as a ripe peach." Father's first words startled him, bursting out like a barked command.

The silence demanded a response. "Is that right?" Perk asked, shouting to overcome Father's near deafness. "How wonderful for her."

"Knows her Bible right the way through."

"I—" The words caught in this throat like a fouled line, and he struggled for land graces. "My compliments on the accomplishment, Miss Bartlett."

The room grew close. Hot, suddenly.

"Keeps a tidy house, I'm told," Father nodded encouragingly to Euphemia.

"Your presence in Marblehead is nothing short of a divine blessing, Captain Creesy." Euphemia spoke as if reading a speech. "My spirits soar to behold you again."

"My—" Perk mouth snapped shut. Gut clenched tight as a fist.

What in damnation was going on here?

"You've been away for years on end, son," Father shouted. With his voice always raised, his tone was impossible to read. "Too long. And it's far past time to start a family."

There was a cross swell that Perk was struggling to read. Behind Father and Euphemia's view, Patience shook her head no. A look of concern as plain on her face as it had been on mother's.

"The good pastor and I have reached an alliance." Father continued, "Tomorrow, the Bartlett and Creesy families will be united. He will make a substantial investment in Creesy & Son Cordage when you will marry his daughter."

Perk's hand was at his belt before he realized why. Before he remembered, there was no knife there to defend himself with.

He'd walked straight into a trap.

"No," he said, sharp as a marlinspike.

There were a lot more things Perk wanted to say. Not a single one was appropriate for mixed company. He barely kept from spitting.

"All due respect to Miss Bartlett," he added through gritted teeth, "But I've earned the right to make my own decisions, Father."

No chance he'd marry that coatless shrew who spoke down her nose at Patience, however much her spirits may soar. But he was furious that the visit he'd hoped for was already ruined before they'd even broken bread.

. . .

THE STEAMER WOULDN'T RETURN until Monday, but maybe he could return to New York sooner by land. He tried to puzzle through a plan, but each step added complication and confusion. Take Sunday's stage to Boston. Monday rail to Providence. Tuesday he could get as far as Stonington. Wednesday a boat back to Manhattan.

Confound it. That did him no good.

The tug would pull the *Oneida* out of her berth Tuesday morning at eleven sharp, timed to make the tide—with or without him. Grinnell had made it plenty clear to Perk that he was replaceable if he failed to return on time.

Only Monday's steamer—direct but for a short stop in Boston—would get him back in time. He'd have to tough it out here in this old house with its peeling paint and sagging roof.

Then an awful thought occurred to Perk.

HE GLANCED AROUND THE PARLOR. The silver candlesticks were gone. A darker patch of wallpaper showed where the gilt mirror had once hung over the fireplace. There was no rug under his boots. It wasn't a small amount of money that Father needed.

A substantial investment, he'd said Bartlett planned to make.

That meant the business was sinking.

Mother had said there was a plan, but always tried to spare Perk from his Father's worst impulses by taking his wrath on herself. He couldn't let her do that to him now, as a grown man.

How much could Father owe? Five hundred dollars? A thousand?

Perk felt the small lump in the inner pocket of his vest—everything he owned in the world—a few half eagles, pieces of eight, and a note from the Second Bank of the United States. Barely more than fifty dollars.

He'd get a bonus if he could find a way to beat the fleet next season, but if things were as dire as he suspected, he'd still never be able to rescue them in time.

Would Mother lose the house? End up in a hovel beyond the Barnegat tanneries without firewood most of the winter? Scrubbing other women's laundry, hands bleeding and raw, begging for scraps of bread?

Oh, hell, Perk thought.

He could never let Mother starve. He tried to work past his revulsion at Euphemia. How much would it matter, a marriage in name only? It galled him to lose an inch to his father, but surely he could bear it for Mother's sake.

He tried to think of it as a business contract. He lived at sea. It was a rare captain's wife who joined her husband on a voyage or two. One or two even made a life of it. But there was precious little danger Euphemia would ever step aboard the *Oneida*.

It was a reasonable trade for Mother's safety.

Patience was shaking her head even more vehemently, as if she knew what he was thinking. He avoided her, trying to work out the excuses he could come up with for staying away from a wife. Storms. Delayed shipments. Repairs. If he sent silks, would Euphemia be satisfied? He imagined she just might.

"Bartlett had one reasonable condition of his investment." Father continued, glaring at Perk as if readying for a fight. "His son-in-law is to run the ropewalk."

Perk tried to recall the Bartlett family. Who was his son-in-law?

Then the weight of it dropped like an anchor.

Perk. Perk was to be Bartlett's son-in-law. He was intended to run the ropewalk.

To never return to the sea.

"No." Perk said. A familiar anger rose in his throat, mixed with a new, vicious urge for survival. "By God's hooks, no!"

"You'd see your mother in the almshouse, would you?" Father shouted, "Send her to an early grave? Is that the kind of man you've become? Too high and mighty to honor his father?"

"No." Perk said, jaw clenched, losing track of which conversational thread he was fighting.

At sea, Perk's hands knew every line. Feet knew every plank. He could set a breathing wall of sails in perfect unison, balancing jib and spanker against the wind's push. At sea, he led a floating island. Twenty-two souls who followed his every command across the treacherous oceans.

On land, Perk would be stuck under his father's thumb, slowly but inexorably reverting to that broken sixteen-year-old boy he'd once been—as if not a single moment had passed since then.

"It's a well-achieved match," Father said, "To a worthy and *virtuous* woman."

Perk read the emphasis, purposely meant to cut Ellen down. His hands clenched until the knuckles whitened, wanting to grab Father by his cravat.

"No," he said, but his voice was softer.

"And a return finally to the business that's always been your birthright. Give it time. You'll thank me."

Perk's chest thrummed like a line pulled three turns too taut. *You'll thank me* is what Father told all his clients just before he set about cheating them.

Mother had told Perk to say no, but how could he leave her destitute?

"No," he whispered, but even he couldn't even hear himself this time.

He retrieved his bag from the corner and set it on his knee long enough to retrieve the jade pendant and hand it wordlessly to Patience. To set the teacups on the dining table for Mother. To leave Father's lacquer box on the side table. To stare at Euphemia, her mouth set in a very unvirtuous 'O' of confusion.

"Tomorrow Pastor Bartlett will conduct your marriage ceremony in the church at nine," Father said. "With a small family meal to follow at his house. I'm told Mrs. Bartlett is preparing a lamb feast."

The floorboards pitched beneath Perk's feet.

He tried to come up with more words, but his voice failed utterly. Finally, he turned and ducked out the door, on his way to find a tavern.

"Half-past nine," Father called out behind him, and his shout echoed down both sides of the winding street. "Your childish games with boats end today."

3

An elbow to the ribs was no way to wake up.

Mathilda had been a fitful sleeper right from the cradle, but Ellen would swear her thrashing had grown worse over the years, making it ever harder to share the bed. The flat, gray dawn revealed her conquest: a full three-quarters of the feather tick mattress—a feat worthy of Napoleon himself.

Frustration nearly drove Ellen to attack her right back. Who was she to doze so peacefully?

Yet her soft little face, usually animated with curiosity or mischief, was so peaceful in slumber. Long lashes rested gently on her cheeks. The white cotton nightcap had pulled askew, so that twists of honey-brown hair and rag curlers poked out like the petals of some strange flower. She'd wear a riot of ringlets to church today.

That child was so like Ellen in some ways—impatient, brash, adventurous—and yet so different in others. Ellen had fought Mama tooth and nail to leave her hair be. To take the lace off her skirts because it caught in the tree branches. To escape tedious conversations about who was courting whom, what new sheet music had come from Leipzig, and the latest efforts to rehabilitate fallen women.

But Mathilda soaked these things up. Seven years old and she already fit into the world far better than Ellen did in her twenties. She tucked a curl behind her sister's ear with a reluctant smile. If they still had Papa's purse, she'd have looked lovely in lace.

ELLEN GLANCED out the window at the pale disc of a sun, half-hidden behind a layer of altostratus clouds. The chop in the harbor showed the wind had shifted from south to southeast, slogging its way counterclockwise to the nor'easter she knew was coming. But it was still a couple of days off. Today would be gusty but dry.

The glimpse of the sea stilled her heart as it always did, putting even yesterday's shock in perspective. She regretted her jealousy. Her selfishness. Even the depth of her past guilt.

Today, she mostly felt happy for Perk. He'd set off as a boy and returned as a captain. She'd seen the change in his newly confident stance. He must be six feet tall now, broad-shouldered and barrel-chested. Though even with the new beard, she'd seen the same face that had always made her smile.

But his choice of Euphemia she didn't follow. Had he molded himself into the social-climbing sycophant his father'd always pushed him to become? What had become of the wild-hearted boy who'd dreamed of far horizons with her?

An unwelcome memory pricked holes in her contentment—the last time she'd seen Perk, when he'd looked at her like she was a bucket of milk gone sour. She tamped it down.

"He deserves to be happy," she whispered to herself, gripping the sill. "If Euphemia gives him that, then I'm glad for their—" She couldn't say marriage, even to herself. "Glad for them."

"YOU'D BETTER BE awake and dressed!" Mama called from behind the door.

Ellen tugged off her nightcap and crawled over Mathilda's now-moving limbs. After six months of reprieve, she knew she was due back at church after yesterday's grim, half-mourning anniversary—an impossible six months since Captain Papa's passing. Propriety said she should have been going to church all along, with Mama and Mathilda, but she suspected she only won the battle to stay home because Mama had ideas turning her reintroduction into an event, so the town would give its misfit a new look, like a butterfly emerging from a chrysalis.

Ellen felt more like a hawk being forced into a dovecote.

One of Mathilda's pinkies twitched in a dream. Still so untroubled. She'd grow up belonging in the world as it was, instead of hoping for one that didn't exist.

Surely Ellen could delay her return until after the wedding. Perk didn't deserve to have his nemesis ruin his big day.

THE DOOR FLEW OPEN. "Up. Now." Mama said. "Ellen, you're to polish the boots. Mathilda, you see if the hens have dropped early eggs. Otherwise, we've only hasty pudding for breakfast."

The cold air seeped into Ellen's skin. "I'll see to the boots," she said, making a mental tally of supplies. Lampblack. Molasses. Goose fat. "But it'll be for the best if I skip the wedding today." Vinegar. Bristle brush. Soft brush. Water bucket.

"No," Mama said. "You too. And do something with that hair of yours. Brace it with carpenter's glue if you must. Mr. Sampson, the cabbage farmer, is coming all the way from Lynn Woods, and is intrigued to meet you."

Ellen started, leaning instinctively toward *The Virtuous Wife* that hid her treasured flower. "But Lynn Woods is *miles* from the sea."

She'd nearly accepted the necessity of marriage. As long as her heart wasn't bound by the union along with her body, she even imagined she could retain some form of independence. But she'd not counted on losing every connection to the ocean as well.

"Must you seek a suitor so far off?"

Mama arched her eyebrows. She didn't need to speak the answer: no one in town would consider it. "You could still attend church here on Sundays," she said. "We'd see each other often enough."

Ellen clutched the nightcap in her fist into a tight ball of cotton. "I'll go next week," she said. "I promise."

Mama thought for a moment, then settled into a spot on the bed between Ellen and Mathilda, resting a hand on each knee as to impart a lesson to both at once.

"I know you don't want to listen to a word I say. And heaven knows the rows I used to have with your papa over your navigation, but every moment you spent on the schooner drew you further from viable marriage prospects. And now here we are. You're a hair's breadth from spinsterhood, is the truth of it. Already well past your prime. And you must listen to me now, my girl, before it's too late."

"Even if that's true," Ellen said with a sigh, "Why must it be today?"

"You're my daughter. My heart." Mama looked away as if trying to hide her sadness, as if Ellen couldn't read it just as clearly in the slump of her shoulders.

"Nothing would have spared you from the grief of your papa's passing, but without the ability to lay him to rest—to say goodbye— you'll always struggle to let him go."

The hollow ache in Ellen's chest squeezed into a tight ball of pain.

"I know how tied you are to Perkins Creesy. All the history you two had, running around like rapscallions. He may have been gone an age, but I don't know that you'll ever move on from him if you don't see him married with your own eyes."

To Euphemia Bartlett, of all people, Ellen thought, cradling the book like a pillow. Had he forgotten Euphemia was the one who'd mocked his worn coat sleeves? Who'd turned up her nose at his calloused hands during dance lessons?

But her sudden anger passed in a moody gust, leaving her with the dull ache of sadness. If Perk could surrender his dreams so completely, perhaps she was a fool for clinging to hers.

Maybe she'd have her chance to apologize after all.

Could she summon the courage?

"I'll never understand your devotion," Mama said, "To the boy who stole you away to Salem, unescorted, then nearly killed the both of you."

Ellen's shame returned in full force, and she realized it was cheating to think she could just tell Perk she was sorry and be done with it. An apology would be meaningless unless she confessed the truth to everyone who mattered.

She'd hoped her great lie would fade away with time. Instead, it etched itself into the stone of collective memory. Telling the truth now would shatter the last modicum of respect anyone had for her.

But wasn't that the same fear that had driven her to lie in the first place?

"It wasn't his fault," Ellen said, approaching the edges of the untruth in a whisper.

"Don't go blaming the weather again. It was wickedness, pure and simple. Whatever he promised to convince you to go on that reckless—"

"—He promised nothing."

Ellen had almost hoped Mama wouldn't hear, but she closed her mouth suddenly, forcing Ellen to continue.

"I'm the one who stole the dory."

There were but a handful of times in Ellen's entire life that she'd seen Mama surprised. Where Ellen could calculate numbers, Mama calculated people. She'd always been able to factor the chaos of Marblehead personalities into tidy equations, and turn them into sense. Yet her hand slipped from Ellen's leg. She blinked hard and fast, as if her eyelashes were at war with each other.

"It was my idea," Ellen continued immediately, terrified she'd lose her nerve. "He was afraid we'd get in trouble. I said no one would ever know. And if Mr. Doyle did notice his dory missing, I promised to take the blame. I wanted—" She'd been so sure of herself, she remembered. Overconfident. "I wanted him to see what was possible."

Mathilda scooted closer, watching Ellen's confession with rare intensity, forcing Ellen to close her eyes in order to finish what she'd started.

"For all he'd dreamed of the ocean, Perk had never been out of Marblehead, had never seen a proper ship—nothing bigger than the shallow draft coasters that can reach our landing. Meanwhile, every day he spent at the ropewalk seemed to hollow him out more. He told me he must become more *practical*. Forget about sailing and help his father grow the cordage company. I felt like I was watching my best friend waste away in front of me, like he had tuberculosis of the spirit. I thought if he could just see what could be, maybe he'd break free and follow his dreams. I'd just gotten such confidence from saving the ship at Cape Henlopen, I was sure I could do anything. Even save Perk."

"I'd been to Salem plenty with Papa, so I knew it was filled with gigantic, ocean-going merchantmen, fresh in from wild adventures and full of dramatic tales. It's naught but four miles from Marblehead across the water—barely an hour's sail on a good breeze, but it might as well be another country."

The beginning of the trip had gone so well. The joy of it loosened her tongue.

"And my plan worked. When we got there, he saw the ships, and the crates printed with Chinese characters, and he saw that sailing wasn't just some fantasy. It was a real thing that real men did. He listened to the stories of typhoons and fire walkers and glowing water, and they let him pet the monkey—"

"What monkey?" Mathilda asked.

Ellen kept her eyes closed, but felt the smile spread across her face. "He was a sweet little guy. Black on the bottom, with a white face and shoulders. Friendly enough, he'd hopped right onto my shoulder, then kept trying to steal the pins out of my hair." Ellen laughed. "They'd picked him up in Rio, I think. Anyway, Perk came alive again, before my very eyes. He said that he wanted to seize each heartbeat of life, not count the hours. He was so—"

Ellen searched for a way to describe his excitement without mentioning their picnic on the grass, the surprise bouquet he'd picked, his unexpected declaration of love, her overwhelming fear of ruining their friendship, or the awkward way she'd ducked from his intended kiss.

Instead, she skipped to the storm. "I was distracted on the return. Didn't see the line squall coming until it hit. We went from near calm to facing a full gale in a bloody—sorry. In a very small rowboat. The dory was massively outmatched. It nearly flipped repeatedly, but Perk—"

She choked on the memory of him working the tiller and the bailing bucket at the same time, even as the waves grew around them until they dwarfed even the spritsail.

"Perk was amazing. He told me exactly where to sit and how far to lean to balance the forces. Sixteen years old and he got us back to the shore in Marblehead Harbor when I swear very few of those professional sailors could have managed it. It was an incredible victory to land safely on the beach at home."

Ellen kept out the part about how she'd thrown her arms around him, ready to kiss him and declare her own feelings right back. Inside the book she clutched lay the one forget-me-not that had managed to ride out that whole storm safely in her pocket.

"Then, suddenly it was if the whole town descended. Furious. Appalled. Even Captain Papa."

"He was worried sick," Mama said. "We both were. Euphemia told everyone you two had gone out *alone* in that dory. That was bad enough. But when the squalls hit and you still weren't back . . ."

Ellen opened her eyes, less afraid of Mama's face than her own memories. "I only knew that Papa was angrier than I'd ever seen him in my life. He was shouting and said it had been a *mistake* to take me out on the *Californian* if it led me to such reckless behavior. How could I even think to follow a boy out to sea? I thought if I told him the truth, that I had actually led the adventure, Papa would never have taken me to sea again."

Ellen took a deep breath and then rushed headlong into the shame before she could change her mind.

"So I lied. I told him Perk surprised me. That I'd only expected to row in the harbor, but he'd sailed us to Salem instead. It was an awful, awful thing I did. I thought I just said it to Papa, but Papa told everyone. And Perk was so angry he never even let me apologize. His father told me for six weeks he refused to see me. The next thing I knew, he'd run off and sailed away as a ship's boy, but he never once answered my letters."

Ellen waited for Mama's reaction. Waited longer. Mathilda's stunned stare was enough to melt her.

"Oh, Ellen," Mama finally said.

Ellen had been prepared for a rebuke, an argument even, but the disappointment in Mama's voice brought another level of pain.

"I'd thought you were so much more practical." Mama shook her head. "Almost drowned the pair of you. Nearly ruined your reputation. And good Lord. Do you know what you did to that boy? His father almost killed him because of that trip."

Ellen jerked back. "What do you mean?"

"We did our best to keep you out of the whole sordid affair," Mama said. "Your Papa and I thought you'd been through enough. But you told everyone he'd kidnapped you . . ."

"Not kidnapped. That's not what I meant. Just—"

"What did you think taking a young girl against her will would mean? The whole town knew his father tied him up in the attic for weeks. Whipped the boy nightly until he finally escaped and ran off."

Ellen gaped. She hadn't thought it possible to feel worse.

She didn't owe Perk an apology. She owed him a blood sacrifice.

"I'll tell everyone it was me," she said, quiet but resolute. "I should have done it a decade ago, but I deserve whatever they do to me."

"You can't do that," Mama said. "It's too late. Can you not see the selfishness of relieving your own conscience by ruining not only the man's wedding, but all of Mathilda's future prospects? No." Mama shook her head. "You're going to go to church today and act as the most virtuous woman you know how to be. You'll congratulate the bride and groom and be on your best behavior. And we'll both hope we can get you married to Mr. Sampson before everything falls to pieces."

———

THE CROWD SWELLED as they drew closer to Marblehead's Old North Church, everyone stepping carefully over cobblestones still slick with dew.

Ellen wondered if Mr. Sampson would have ear hair. If he'd have a gentle temperament or wake with a sneer. If she could learn to love cabbage. She tried to tell herself it didn't matter, that survival was survival, but her heart knew better.

Her stays grew viselike.

She searched for Perk's distinctive stride as Mathilda slipped her hand into hers, icy but solid, and gave her three quick squeezes—their secret code for solidarity.

"Which way is Salem?" Mathilda asked, and for once, Ellen was glad for the distraction from her own thoughts.

"Just around the point is a larger harbor," she answered, pointing. Was he watching her point? "Salem's just the other side of it."

"Do all sailors get monkeys?"

Ellen managed a laugh. "Not all of them," she said. "But sometimes there's a monkey or two aboard." She squeezed her sister's hand back, three times. "Especially if the ships have come from Brazil or India."

The last steps up the hill and inside the church became a confusion of jostling and crowding. Mr. Lee was in a capital mood. Mrs. Washburn's nostrils flared from some unknown slight. Mrs. Connelly tried to relate some story involving a butter churn but kept laughing too hard to finish it.

When Ellen finally took a seat in her box pew on the southwest wall of the nave, Mama motioned for others to join. She was merely being polite, making room for the large crowd, but when the Jones sisters squeezed into Captain Papa's empty seat, Ellen felt it like a stinging betrayal. Worse, it meant Mathilda got stuck by herself all the way at the end of the pew, but it was the last thing Ellen was going to fuss about today.

She glanced at Euphemia, in her usual box at the front, wearing the same peacock-blue dress as yesterday. After all this time, after all their battles, Ellen thought, the one who'd always acted superior had been so all along.

She wondered how they'd reconnected. When they'd fallen in love. Was it her piety? Her singing? Perk didn't care about such things, she thought. But then, what did she know of Perk anymore?

She reached for a prayer book and opened it to hide her face. Then she practiced the smile she'd greet him with—not too cheery for an apology, not too dour for a wedding. The tightness in her jaw told her that her smile was coming out as more of a snarl.

She put the book down.

"Back row on the left," Mama whispered. "In the gray coat."

ELLEN FROZE, not wanting to see Mr. Sampson as a real, breathing person who—if she was lucky enough—would soon own her body, if not her soul. But Mama arched her brows, so Ellen forced a smile to her face—lest he be watching—and turned around.

There were two gray coats. Neither was over the age of seventy.

Neither made her heart sing. She realized she didn't care which one of them it was. One Mr. Sampson would do as well as the other.

She returned her gaze to the front and held herself in her closest approximation to a demure position as spirited chatter filled the nave with a hum of expectation. But to Ellen, the air already felt stale with musty wet wool.

Mother smoothed her skirts. Henry bounced little Hannah on his knee and Mrs. Doyle licked her hand to smooth Lindon's unruly hair.

The whole time, twelve rows up, Euphemia kept her eyes fixed properly in her lap. No fidgeting. No whispering. She may as well have been a blue-clad marble statue.

The very picture of a good girl, Ellen thought. No mud-stained hems or wild hair. No ragged breaths from sprinting down the lane. Her mind bent to pleasing others, not puzzling through spherical trigonometry, just like Mama had always said.

In the end, the good girl had won.

THE FIRST CLANG of the church bell gave Ellen a start, but then she let the resonant notes echo through her chest. Paul Revere himself had cast that very bell, and somehow that had always seemed special. As if the sound it produced could connect her, however tenuously, to the courage of its caster.

Pastor Bartlett waited at his pulpit, smiling at his dutiful daughter as the conversations faded out like snuffed candles. Sarah Jones's elbow dug into Ellen's ribs as she twisted around to stare at the doors.

Ellen took a deep breath and did the same.

The whole church waited for Perk to appear.

The last harmonic tones of the bell decayed into a weighty silence.

Would his eyes still crinkle at the corners when he smiled? Would he still have that slight swagger in his walk? The years may have transformed him into someone who could court a pastor's daughter, but she remembered how he'd once paced the docks like a caged animal, looking for any way to escape such society.

Finally, the door swung open, but it wasn't Perk who walked through it.

Mrs. Creesy wore the telltale squint of a headache. Next to her, Patience took her hand and they strode forward, resolutely, to the family box. At her breast, Patience wore a small pin of preserved myrtle—common enough for a wedding—but woven with dried everlasting flowers.

Ellen's mouth flew open. Why would Patience pair symbols for undying love and eternal sorrow together?

Mr. Creesy burst in next, chest heaving, shoulders hunched like a beaten dog. The same man who'd once broken three of Perk's ribs for missing a Sunday service.

He could barely meet Pastor Bartlett's eye.

What on earth had happened to Perk?

Ellen was half out of her seat by the time Mama grabbed her skirt and pulled her back down.

"Eyes forward," Mama hissed. "Don't forget you're being evaluated."

Ellen returned to the black tunnel of her bonnet, wondering for all the world, what looks Mr. Creesy and Pastor Bartlett were giving each other. Robbed of sight, she listened intently but heard nothing beyond a lone infant gently fussing in the back. Otherwise, not a cough, not a shuffle, not a creak.

Eventually, she heard Mr. Creesy stride down the center aisle to his box, boot heels punishing the floorboards with each step.

Then something caused a collective shuffling of feet, and a dramatic thump echoed through the church.

Ellen looked up at the pulpit. Bartlett had flung open his weighty Bible. He was preparing to conduct a Sunday sermon after all.

There would be no wedding.

Ellen swallowed her surprise. Mathilda shifted in her seat. Henry bounced Hannah.

All waited breathlessly for whatever was to follow.

"Today, we bear witness to a grievous act of cowardice," Bartlett thundered, "And are thus all injured as a community, robbed of the opportunity to witness the lifelong vows and glad tidings of a wedding celebration."

Ellen frowned. One could call Perk many things—controlling, pig-headed, temperamental—but coward was about the last word one could ever bend to fit him.

What could have happened?

She stole a look at Euphemia, as if she might have the answer. The bonnet wings shielded her face, but the slump of her shoulders revealed an ache of grief. Ellen knew the feeling far too well. She'd never have thought it possible to feel sorry for Euphemia, but had never anticipated such public humiliation for her either.

"The marriage which should have taken place today, we can all agree, would have been a pure and just example of God's work," Bartlett said. "So when a virtuous angel of a woman is so cruelly cast aside, we accept the only viable explanation. It is not Our Lord's hand at work, but His opposite. The dark shadow we must be ever diligent to banish from the safety of our flock, lest we be pulled from our path of righteousness.

"From today to eternity, Captain Josiah Perkins Creesy is to be shunned by this community for his weakness in the face of the devil. He will certainly face the peril of divine judgement." Bartlett's voice vibrated, as if he was barely holding on to the fury that wanted to explode out from under him.

"But when a promising son of Marblehead is ruined before our very eyes, when he is pulled into the fires of wickedness, we must be more than shocked. We must ask ourselves whose hands the devil has been using to destroy us from within."

Ellen looked back at the pulpit and was startled to find Bartlett's eyes locked on her, trapping her with his stare, his face twisted in fury.

The heat rose in her cheeks. What did she have to do with a missing groom?

"Who could tempt such an otherwise stalwart a man away from such a perfect example of the innate qualities of womankind: modesty, silence, and steadfast devotion as Miss Euphemia Bartlett?" The pastor turned to indicate his daughter and Ellen breathed a sigh of relief. Bartlett's stare had been a fluke. Merely her guilty imagination at work.

"Who but an unnatural seductress? One among us—here in this very congregation—who's not only rejected her God-given nature, she's rebelled against the very idea of natural obedience. Someone we all know to be the closest confidant of Mr. Creesy. Someone who most certainly whispered her vile temptations into his ear."

His eyes returned to Ellen. This time they stayed there.

"I need not even speak her name, for you all know the woman who has lived among us not with blessed humility, but the stain of pride. Who's striven not for the glory of beauty or the selfless nurturing that is the highest achievement of her sex, but shockingly bent her efforts toward selfish ambition."

Ellen sat ramrod straight against his glare, desperately trying to add up the pieces that might cause Bartlett to attack her so violently out of nowhere.

Because Captain Papa could no longer protect her?

Because she'd confronted him about Fluke?

Because he felt despair over his daughter's pain, or humiliation over his own plans being rejected? That would explain his vehemence, but how did it connect to her if she hadn't even spoken to Perk in ten years?

"—Our Lord left us explicit instructions in First Timothy, chapter two, verses eleven and twelve in order to keep us safe from such wickedness: 'I suffer not a woman to teach, nor to usurp authority over the man, but *to be in silence.*' And again in First Corinthians, He tells us, 'The head of the woman is the man.' And Ephesians: 'Wives, submit yourselves unto your own husbands, as unto the Lord.' "

Suddenly, it occurred to Ellen that Bartlett didn't know she'd betrayed Perk's trust. Didn't realize Perk actually hated her more than anyone. That she was actually the last person on earth who could have prevented Perk from marrying Euphemia.

For the pastor, who else but Euphemia's nemesis for all these years, however unintended the rivalry may have been from Ellen's side. Who else but the harlot who'd once gone off with Perk all the way to Salem—*unaccompanied?* Who else but the Jezebel who dared speak out against her own pastor in the market.

"God has warned us that a woman's sole task on this earth is to obey!" he thundered. "Not to pervert her mind with learning. Not to fraternize unashamedly with boys. Not to overexert her head with mathematics, or bewitch an otherwise promising man into the most vile, the most unforgivable betrayal of his bride on the very day of her wedding."

Ellen gripped the prayer book until her knuckles ached. Bartlett was burning her alive for a sin she'd not committed, but there was a worse sin she *had* committed years ago. A different betrayal but just as unforgivable. One she did deserve to burn for.

Ellen bent her head in contrition and allowed Bartlett's abuse to rain down on her, allowed some of it to even pierce her heart.

All her attempts to become agreeable had come to ruin. If Mr. Sampson were watching—and he would have had to be drunk or dead not to—he wouldn't dare speak a word to her today or any other day. After today, no one in all of Essex county would give her the time of day. If she was ever to get married, she'd have to seek a groom somewhere out past the Kansas territories.

But all the while, she worried for Perk. The boy she'd known would have—*had, in fact*—braved a literal tempest rather than let down someone he cared about.

Wherever he was right now, she was certain he must be suffering. He was such a powerful, ambitious, hardworking, brawling, competitive person. And yet, there was also a gentle soul inside him. A tender heart. A wistful dreamer who'd so often been forced to crush his own desires.

"A willful woman brings disgrace to our community!"

Bartlett had moved past her authentic shame to his same old, tired pronouncements. Ellen tried to catch a glimpse of Mathilda, but the bonnet prevented the view. A part of her ached to reach across the Jones sisters to offer three quick squeezes, but that would only draw more attention.

"So let us be reminded what virtues we must instill in our women. A virtuous woman is modest!" Bartlett yelled. "A virtuous woman is silent!"

That's because any woman who spoke their mind would tell you what a vainglorious windbag you are, Ellen thought.

Where was Perk? What had gone wrong?

She thought of him as a boy, braving an anthill with a stick for a sword, shouting "Give me liberty or give me death!"

Perhaps she and Perk had both been prisoners all along, just in different types of jails.

Bartlett had called him a coward, but maybe his absence today wasn't cowardice at all. Perhaps he'd not been sweet on Euphemia after all. What if his absence was actually the utmost of bravery—fighting for what mattered most to him?

"A virtuous woman doesn't fatigue her spirit with books, but looketh well to the ways of her household. She eateth not the bread of idleness," Bartlett thundered.

Idleness is what the pastor had called it when Ellen was nine and he discovered she'd learned trigonometry. If the girl had extra time for such idleness, he'd argued with Papa, it would be better spent doing charity work. When he learned she'd actually corrected the boys' teacher, he'd elevated his concern to an 'unnatural' behavior.

"Don't be ridiculous," Captain Papa had said to the neighbors later, as unperturbed as if someone had decreed the sky to be orange. "Where do you think her genius comes from, if not the Lord Himself?"

If Captain Papa had been here today, he would have made a quiet joke after services to defuse the tension. To counteract Bartlett's vehemence by showing the outlandishness of its frame. But Captain Papa wasn't here. He wasn't even at his polished gravestone out back. He was somewhere underneath the North Atlantic, off the coast of Savannah to her best calculation, forever sailing beneath the waves.

For the rest of the sermon, Ellen kept wishing she had a sword of her own with which to battle a seeable, knowable enemy. Not these tricky shadows, not these thundering pronouncements.

The Bartlett's needles of fear and fury had tattooed an indelible decision onto her heart. A woman's sole task on this earth, he'd said, was to obey.

She refused to agree.

Her only weapon against such a prison was as ironic as it was powerful.

Silence.

Come what may, she would never, ever, vow obedience to anyone. Not a husband. Not an employer. Not even a four-star general.

When Bartlett's fury was spent, the seemingly endless sermon finally came to a close. As the congregation rose, Ellen donned her coat—then fell back onto the pew.

Perk had escaped.

From Marblehead. From the ropewalk. From his father. He'd really done it. Defied them all.

Whatever the reason for his choice not to marry Euphemia, he'd finally broken free of the weight of all their expectations for good. And this was the worst of the results? That people he didn't like, didn't like him back?

Could there be hope for her wild heart yet?

Church emptied faster than usual. No one wanted to linger long in discussion with Bartlett on this particular day, and Ellen least of all. She reached for Mathilda's shoulder, to shield her from whatever scowls or shouts the pastor may have left to give, but there was no shoulder.

No Mathilda.

Ellen spun around, searching through the crowd. Mathilda was nowhere. She peeked behind the pew. Not there. Pushed her way past everyone to get outside.

No Mathilda.

And then a terrifying thought struck her.

She knew exactly where her sister had gone.

4

____

No matter how hard Perk tried to focus on the harbor in front of him, he found his gaze drawn back to the white steeple, thrust into the mackerel sky like an accusing finger. Walking along the sand, he waited for the bells.

Three times this morning he'd started up that hill. To remind them of his refusal, explain his reasons, or bend to their scheme? Even he didn't know. Three times his feet had refused to carry him further.

The congregation would be assembled by now, their Sunday best pressed and proper, waiting for him—hope wearing thin with each empty minute. Mother. Euphemia.

Ellen.

What must she be thinking? Surely she knew him better than to think he'd ever stoop so low as to court such a—oh, but who cared what Ellen thought. Her opinion meant nothing to him now.

Finally, the church bells began their somber count, each bronze note falling like a hammer blow. Seven. Eight. Nine. The sound reached down the hill, echoed across the water, vibrated in his chest.

The final toll marked the turn of the tide. There'd be no going back.

Father would consider Perk dead to him. The town would call him gutless as a jellyfish. Ellen would think—whatever Ellen would think. To whatever extent Marblehead had been his home, it was no longer.

Monday's ferry couldn't come soon enough. He hoped he could merely slip away like the morning mist, leaving no trace behind.

Until then, he paced the shoreline, practically wearing holes into his boots, trying to figure out how to make three years' salary in a single voyage—before Mother lost her house.

THERE WAS ONLY one way he knew to make such easy money. But Grinnell & Minturn were both Quakers and—as far as Perk was aware—ran the only tea trading firm in all of New York that strictly forbid dealing in opium.

The Protestant Astors and Delanos were not so discerning. Nor were the Aspinwalls or the Lows. Hell, the Brits practically turned it into a national sport.

While the East India Company took on chests full of the sticky black balls in Bengal, the Americans traded first with Turkish Smyrna. After that, the process was identical. When the opium-stuffed ships reached the Pearl River delta outside Canton, they unloaded their smuggled goods in the dead of night onto moored hong merchant vessels—in abject defiance of Chinese Law.

Perk had always been grateful to avoid such seedy activities. But given his mother's desperate finances, he couldn't argue with one essential fact. By the time they'd reached the official anchorage in Whampoa, the ships—and their captains—had already taken on five times the silver they'd make on the tea itself.

Was it time to reconsider his reluctance?

If Captain Forbes could line his pockets in the process, why not Perk? Captain Dumaresque didn't mind the extra income. Nor did Captains Low or Hingham. Even jolly old Captain Nat had a hand in it.

Captain Waterman had even been as flagrant in his dealings as the Brits last summer—so much so that exasperated Chinese officials had threatened to shut down the entire Western trading complex. It would never happen, of course. There was too much money to be made from trade on both sides, and no one in their right minds would scuttle a lifeboat to drown a rat.

But Chinese indignation with the sordid business had grown vehement. And it led Perk to realize there was someone else unscrupulous enough to argue that blood money from a poisonous trade was a righteous path to a noble family legacy.

His father.

That thought was enough to make Perk seasick that he'd even considered it.

But what to do for Mother? She'd refused to take his fifty dollars. He'd tried time and again. For that matter, what to do about his own precarious situation?

"I'm still hoping you'll pull this off, Creesy," Grinnell had warned him, "But I can't afford another disastrously late arrival in New York. So you'll have to prove your abilities on the way out to Canton this time if you want to be the one to bring the ship home. I'll give you a reasonable 130 days to make it from Sandy Hook to Whampoa. Do so and you'll keep your post at least for the return. But fail that and Mr. Austin carries letters that empower him—on condition of 131 or more days to complete the outbound voyage—to take over command of the *Oneida*. You'd be left to make your own way home."

Perk couldn't argue he'd had a run of bad luck because he knew two things without a doubt. First, that he could drive a ship harder and faster than any man alive in equal conditions. Second, that something was very wrong with the conditions.

On the last trip, he'd sailed right out of the trades and into dead-still air. The time before that, he'd fought against the westerlies around Good Hope for a month without an inch of progress to show for it. And the time before that, he still didn't know what exactly had gone wrong, but he'd come in almost dead last.

Meanwhile, the other captains faced the same oceans, the same weather systems, and beat him by a mile. He knew it was due to his weakness in strategy. There was something they all did far better than him, and it was something related to navigation.

He'd hoped to be assigned a crack navigator for his first mate. Instead, he was given Thomas Austin, who—for all his family connections—couldn't find north with both hands.

Perk knew he may not be a captain much longer.

Now, as he walked the sand, Perk watched a dory head into the harbor with its spritsail flying—too far away for him to see who was brave enough to skip church on a Sunday. But as he remembered the feel of holding a tiller and sheet, a deep burn spread through his forearms. He hadn't realized how much he missed the purity of sailing itself. Being able to put his whole self into the kind of task that he was made for.

Becoming one with the vessel, the wind, and the water. Making the most of every moment of the race. Knowing the *Oneida* wanted her main royal sheet trimmed a fraction here, that she'd gladly carry her mizzen topsail in a higher gust there, despite the strain on wood and canvas. He knew how to turn a barnacle-encrusted old packet into a racehorse, and she stepped up to his touch.

But for all of that love, he hated the captain's confounded job of deciding which course to steer.

He found his fingers locked into fists and shook them loose, slapping his palms against his thighs until the blood flowed again. Flogging the booby. He almost laughed. Father thought he knew every fiber of the maritime world, but Perk would bet his last dollar he didn't know that.

Then the thought of Father made his chest coil tight again. Coming all this way, finally ready to forgive the past, only to have the man try to bind him in a spider's web. As if he was still the sixteen-year-old boy whose skin remembered his fists, his belt, that dark attic—

No. He was a man now. More than that, he was bigger than Father. A head taller. Far more experienced.

Had Father ever felt the cool shadow of a pagoda? Let bird's nest soup slide across his tongue? Filled his belly with Osmanthus wine and lungs with incense? Had his ears ever felt the vibrations of a zither as a woman in a silk qipao moved like flowing water before him?

But even that memory—sweet as summer rain in the moment—brought both pain and consequences far beyond any hangover. Perk had crossed a line he'd sworn never to breach. That Father would have clapped him on the back in approval only made the bile rise faster in his throat.

Fei Yen, she'd called herself—Flying Swallow. He remembered her at the window, yearning for a bird's freedom. He'd laid the silver in her palm, acted as gently as he knew how, but it was just a minor slip of her smile when she thought he was sleeping, that revealed the truth. By touching her, he'd trapped her further. Lashed himself to her pain forever. The shame clung to his skin like spray, an obligation he could never fully discharge.

The thought turned even the clean ocean breeze to ashes. No, Father had never known a flower boat, but he would have frequented one without regrets. Perk had—that single time—and the weight of it still pressed against his conscience.

He drew the brackish air deep into his chest, forcing out the leaden weight of shame and letting fiery anger flood his veins instead.

Father had wanted to cage him into binding rope, to waste away at a desk in that stifling factory, choking on manila dust, while the eternal grinding of the jack wheel and its wooden teeth wore grooves into his brain. Twisting and twisting and twisting until Perk's muscles forgot the feel of open water.

But the fury moved through him, unbidden as the tides, and he came back to shame. He should have at least had the courage to face the consequences of his decision today.

PERK GLANCED at the pale disc of sun through the gauzy clouds, high enough that whatever Bartlett had improvised as a service would finish soon.

If there was a God, Perk felt sure He wasn't trapped in that old coffin of a church or its musty doctrines. He lived in every fair wind, in the scattered diamonds of stars, in the endless pulse of the sea. When Perk searched for God, he didn't lift his eyes skyward, but found the seam between sea and sky.

For him, God lived in the horizon line.

The dunes on the other side of the harbor blocked that sacred line now, but it waited for him, just beyond the fleet at anchor. Past the restless seabirds and the stone fingers of the jetty. Past that dory, spinning like a compass gone mad.

A grunt of amusement escaped him at the sight. Someone clearly couldn't handle their canvas. It was an open twelve-footer, just like the one he and Ellen—but he forced that thought away. Some things were better left buried.

The boat wheeled in circles, shipping water each time the waves caught it beam-to. He tracked the flogging canvas, the lines whipping violently against the thwarts, and his laugh caught in his throat. The vessel lurched like a punch-drunk boxer, each wave threatening to capsize her. It wouldn't be but a half-bell before it sank at this rate.

Then a tiny figure rose above the gunwale and his gut clenched like he'd been struck.

A child. A girl-child. Barely big enough to reach the tiller, much less muscle it against the chop.

THE WARMTH DRAINED from his body, every nerve screaming

danger as he measured the distance to the nearest rowboat left on shore—a quarter cable down the beach.

His legs were moving before his mind caught up.

"Stay down!" The words tore from his throat, but the wind snatched them away. The mast could come down on top of her. The flailing sheets could snap her arm or crush her skull. If she leaned the wrong way, the boat could turtle in an instant.

He reached the rowboat, his lungs burning, and found the oars shipped tidily under the thwarts. The skiff had been left well high of the tide, moored to a rock, and after freeing the painter he threw his shoulder against the stern, muscles straining to push it toward the harbor. The weight fought him, yielding only an arm's span at a time.

Two fathoms from the water, he tried signaling the girl again, his arm sweeping low to urge her down.

His stomach clenched—he couldn't tell if she understood. The mast carved another circle through the air, the sheets whistling past where her head had been.

Perk heaved against the skiff's stern once more, then staggered as it suddenly lurched forward into the water. He felt another body next to his. Someone else had seen her peril. Spray stung his face as they both leapt in. Without looking, he knew he'd be the stronger rower. Many had tried to beat him in Pearl River races. Most had failed.

He shifted to the forward thwart, tracking the dory while his companion wrestled the oars into place with a fluid efficiency that struck deep chords of memory. No wasted motion, no fumbling with the locks—just the clean snap of wood meeting brass that matched the rhythm in Perk's head.

When he glanced at the harbor behind him to fix the heading, the handles were pressed into his waiting palms, as if his helper knew exactly how he'd want them positioned.

Perk threw his weight into each pull until his shoulders screamed. Twelve strokes in, he lifted his chin to thank the stranger who moved like his shadow and saw a black bonnet. His arms kept their rhythm from pure habit while his mind stumbled, trying to grasp why a man would wear—

Then Ellen looked up from beneath the brim, and his world tilted sideways. He dropped the oars. At speed, both blades flew back and nailed him in the chest with a thud.

"What's the matter with you? Row, blast it!" Ellen shouted.

PERK ROWED. He rowed and rowed because it was all he could do. Ellen sat as she always had—slightly to starboard to balance his stronger pull to larboard.

Questions crowded Perk's throat like bitter water, but he swallowed them back. There was only the burn in his shoulders, the bite of wood against his calloused palms, and the ghost of a hundred summer evenings when they'd moved through the water just like this, reading each other's rhythms as naturally as breathing.

He looked past his shoulder at the girl, his arms burning with each stroke. They'd covered half the distance, maybe twelve boat-lengths. "Stay down!" He bellowed, the words tearing from deep in his chest. This time, the girl disappeared below the gunwales.

He shifted his gaze to Ellen. She was single-minded and efficient as always, but a quiet terror flickered in the hazel eyes he knew so well.

"Keep rowing!" Strain etched lines around her mouth. "That's my sister!"

"Aye," Perk grunted.

Sister? Since when? His jaw clenched, muscles bunching as he dug deeper, feeling the water's resistance through the oars. The chop rose higher now, each wave sending cold spray through his sodden jacket.

"Don't look back," Ellen commanded, her focus beyond his shoulder. "It's slowing you down. Head two more points to starboard."

"One point," Perk forced out between labored breaths, lungs heaving.

"Tide's going out," she said, eyes fixed on the dory. "There's a three-knot current setting you north. Two points to starboard."

Perk yielded, throwing more weight behind the left oar until he felt the boat's heading shift.

The current explained how the girl had gotten into such trouble in the first place. The full moon meant a vicious ebb. If she'd merely slipped the painter, the tide would have yanked her into deep water like a fish on a line.

"Good. One more point. Two hundred yards out." Ellen said.

Despite her worry, her voice steadied him. Having her call the direction let him focus his muscles on rowing, every sinew driving into the oars. The boat's motion confirmed her read of the current—the same current Perk might have felt in his bones earlier if his lungs hadn't been heaving like bellows.

"That's it. Straight on. One fifty. You know how to do this, Perk."

She knew who he was, then. He'd assumed but not known for sure. The thought slipped away under the white-hot weight in his shoulders.

He kept himself strong, worked alongside his crew daily, but this kind of rowing belonged to another life. His lower back screamed louder than his arms—those old racing victories had come from knowing the real power flowed up from the spine, not out from the shoulders.

A swell slammed the larboard bow, drenching him again and nearly wrenching the oar from his left hand. His fingers locked around the wood like iron bands.

"One point to starboard now. A hundred yards," Ellen said. Her words fell steady as a pendulum, and the pain faded. The cold spray, the blistering handle—all of it vanished. There was only the pull.

Ellen stood now, her legs finding their balance in the pitching boat natural as an old salt, her hands cupped around her mouth.

"Stay down!" Ellen shouted to her sister. "We're nearly there!"

Perk pulled harder, eyes shut against the spray, feeling the wooden oars flex with each stroke. The next moments would be the most dangerous—two boats colliding in rough seas could mean broken bones or worse. He'd seen enough rescue attempts end in disaster.

"Straight on. Fifty yards," Ellen called, her voice steady despite the dread in her eyes. She'd already prepared a rope with a weighted knot at the end, sized perfectly for small hands to catch. "I'll count down the last twenty strokes, then we'll drift down on her from windward."

Perk opened his mouth to argue—giving orders was his role now. Had been for years. But the simple rightness of her plan settled into his bones like a familiar weight. He nodded his assent.

"I'll throw the line to Mathilda," Ellen said. "If the waves push us too close, you row us away. Too far, I'll pull us in."

Perk leaned into the oars. Ellen drew a breath, then counted down the last strokes. "Nineteen. Eighteen."

Perk was grateful he could focus on the efficiency of getting the most out of each one.

"Eleven. Ten."

The rough wood bit into his palms with each pull. Cold water had soaked through to his bones, each breath visible in the wind. But a strange calm spread from his gut outward—a forgotten comfort he couldn't name. He pushed the feeling aside, let his body do what it knew how to do.

"Four. Three."

His last strokes turned them into the wind's teeth. Ellen found her balance at the stern, called instructions to Mathilda, then threw the weighted line into the spinning boat. Her aim was perfect—those same sure hands that used to outthrow him clear across Miller's Pond.

Perk held the boat steady against the wind, keeping them just upwind of the spinning dory. Ellen told Mathilda to hold fast as she secured a line around Mathilda's oarlock since no one could safely reach the bow.

Smart thinking, Perk realized. He had been ready to leave the other dory to its fate. Towing her sideways was a novel idea. She'd fight him like a stubborn mule, but she'd follow.

Ellen leaned out over the stern, and Perk shifted his feet to take the riskier position. But before he could step forward, she'd already hauled the frightened, shivering little girl into the boat.

When Perk finally saw the young girl's face, it was like staring at a ghost.

5

———

Ellen pulled Mathilda over the transom and into the rowboat, hugging her tight against her chest. Her sister's cheeks had gone nearly blue, and Ellen sat on the thwart facing the stern, cocooning the shaking girl with her whole body.

It was only once the rescue was complete that Ellen suddenly felt the full terror of what could have happened. Her heart hammered against her ribs, blood rushed in her ears.

Some part of her that had long been sleepwalking through the past six months now felt intensely awake.

The fierce protectiveness that surged through her was raw. Primal. Mathilda was hers to protect, and she'd nearly failed. The girl hadn't felt this small and fragile even as an infant.

Then again, as a baby, she'd never tried to sail a bloody boat all by herself.

The sodden weight of Ellen's clothing dragged at her movements. Salt water dripped from her coat sleeves as she pushed her sister to arm's length, studying her for injuries. "Are you hurt?"

Mathilda looked back at her, wide-eyed, as if she didn't have the words to describe what had just happened to her. She bit her lip, but didn't cry. Finally, she shook her head.

Ellen was partially relieved, but while her sister had many admirable qualities, silence wasn't one of them. There was some kind of injury, just not to her body.

"That was so—" she fought for the right word. Stupid! Reckless! Dangerous!

"So brave of you," Perk said from the bow.

Mathilda peered around Ellen's shoulder at the stranger, then glanced up at her sister with questioning eyes. "I wasn't scared," she said. Then, despite her chin shaking with cold, the hint of a smile crept across her face. "A little scared."

"Come here. Let's warm you up," Ellen said, twisting around on the seat to face Perk at the bow and heaving Mathilda up and over the thwart to the safer center of the boat. She's okay, she kept telling herself, but it took her ages to unbutton her coat because she couldn't get her fingers to stop shaking.

Perk turned the rowboat toward the shore again, expertly pulling with his right hand while pushing with his left. Then the powerful sweep of his oars propelled them forward, clean and neat, until the line to the dory grew taut and tempered their momentum. Despite the chop, Ellen noticed, Perk set just the right distance between the two boats. As expert a rower now as he'd always been, though he'd grown far more powerful.

The other dory tugged unhappily against its new leash, and the wind-whipped waves continued to lash at them. She realized he'd still have to row fast to reach the shore before one of the boats swamped.

Ellen pulled Mathilda into her lap, rubbed each of her starfish hands between her palms, and then enveloped her sister inside her coat. "I was worried sick, little one," she said. "When I realized where you'd gone—" As she rubbed warmth back into her sister's limbs, she found that even half-grown, the girl still fit perfectly in her arms.

"Pastor Bartlett was shouting at you so loud." Mathilda said.

Perk threw Ellen a questioning glance, but she waved it off. Too much to explain under the best circumstances, and she wouldn't have wanted to anyway.

"So I tried to go see the monkey instead, but the boat wouldn't behave."

Tears of relief surprised Ellen, spilling over her cheeks. Of course not, she wanted to say. Don't you try that ever again! But what would that create? Another Euphemia?

"Everything new feels hard at first," she finally said, rubbing heat back into Mathilda's legs, through her skirts. "It helps to have someone teach you how to sail properly."

"Did Papa teach you?" Her teeth chattered.

Ellen almost choked on memories of the careful lessons she'd received. How to use the tiny hairs on her cheeks to feel the direction of the wind. How to capture its invisible and stunning power in the trim of a sail—pulled tight on a beat, loose on a reach—finding the perfect orientation by letting the sail out until the forward edge luffed, then pulling back until it stopped. How to tack with gusto and jibe with caution. Her hand on the tiller. His hand over hers.

But it wasn't Captain Papa's hand.

"No, LITTLE ONE," she said, only able to speak of the before times if she didn't look at Perk. "It was actually this man who taught me to sail. Back when we weren't much older than you. His name is Perkins —that is—I believe it's now Captain Creesy."

Out of the corner of her eye, she glimpsed Perk briefly take his right hand off the oar to tip his cap. "Nice to meet you, Miss Mathilda. I can see the resemblance to your sister."

Ellen wasn't sure if he meant the heart shape of her face, her adventurous spirit, or her idiotic recklessness, but she immediately felt self-conscious. Everything she could say to Mathilda got caught behind a thousand layers of meaning.

He taught me how to sail. I've missed him. I'm furious at him for never once writing. I utterly deserved his rejection—and a lot worse.

"Without him, I don't know what would have happened to you today," she finally said. "I just can't imagine—" Her throat closed up before she could say more, and she shook with fear after the fact.

"Nothing to it," Perk said. "Just a little Sunday row in the park." But even he looked exhausted, straining to pull both boats as the wind picked up.

The rhythmic pull of the oars drew Ellen's gaze to Perk's shoulders, broader now than in her memories. Each stroke revealed the quiet strength in his movements, so different from the gangly boy she remembered. A bead of sweat traced its way slowly down his forehead.

When he glanced up and caught her eyes, she glanced away, heat rising in her cheeks despite the cold.

Mathilda squirmed in her lap, looking between them with curiosity. Ellen silently prayed she wouldn't comment on how close they sat, how their knees nearly touched each time Perk leaned forward. The impropriety of it all would set tongues wagging, but in this moment, she couldn't bring herself to move.

"It was the exciting kind of scared," Mathilda said, perhaps for her own benefit.

An ice-cold wave leapt over the gunnel and buried Ellen's lap—Mathilda included. She searched the bilge for a bailing bucket, but found none. Nearly a foot of water already sloshed back and forth between their feet.

Without Perk, Ellen would never have known that she loved to sail. Would never have begged Captain Papa to take her with him to Boston, Providence, and New York. Wouldn't have pestered her father to teach her navigation, or discovered the magic formulas that leveraged the infinite scope of the heavens to place one tiny schooner on the vast plane of an ocean. Mathematics as invisible and as real a power as the wind itself.

"Your cheeks are all red," Mathilda said to her.

Ellen did her best to ignore the comment. "How is it you were here?" She found the courage to ask. Perk looked confused for a moment, and she realized her question could have meant anything. Here in Marblehead. Here in the states. "On the shore, I mean. You weren't—"

Good Lord, the wedding! How could she—? She studied each button of her soaked boots. "I didn't see you at church."

"I was walking," he answered, voice tight, words as succinct as ever.

Still not ready to meet his eye, she watched the oars. One stroke. Two. An adept rower, the water eddied in tight circles around the blade before he raised it out of the water and sent it reaching behind him. Perk had an invisible power all his own.

The distance of half a lifetime descended in the silence. She held Mathilda like a pillow against her heart and braved another glance.

Perk's shoulders tensed with each stroke, his coat glistening with spray.

"Had a difference of opinion with the old man," Perk said, generously smoothing the awkwardness.

Ellen realized that she'd been right in church. That Perk hadn't been a coward at all, but a man of utmost conviction and iron nerve.

She thought of how Perk's father had always loomed over his life like a black rain cloud, flattening his spirit. His father must have engineered the match for him the same way Mama had tried for her. Somehow she'd always pictured men having so many more choices.

She weighed the weight of the words she needed to speak to him, and the opportunity, finally, for doing so.

I'm sorry for ruining your life.

I'm sorry that your father almost killed you because of me.

I'm sorry I was so weak.

THEN MATHILDA SHIFTED in her lap and she decided to wait for a better moment. Maybe when they could be alone.

"Well," she said, trying to convey an optimism she didn't possess. "You're a hero now. I'm sure rescuing a young girl will put you in his highest esteem—"

Was she blushing?

Perk barked a laugh. "If getting my own command didn't sway him—"

He cut himself off.

Even now, Ellen realized, Perk chose not to brag in front of her. Of all the people who deserved it.

She reached deep to flash him her warmest smile. Not a plastered false cheer, but one that came from a deeper well of feeling. From the authentic truth.

"You deserve every bit of it, Perk."

He wavered in his rhythmic rowing—just a hair—but enough for her to know. Under that heavy brown beard and bearlike shoulders, he was still the Perkins she knew. The strongest, most capable, most hurt little boy she'd ever known.

His face grew redder, and she wondered if he was thinking of a disappointed father, a jilted bride, or the devastating betrayal that had come between them, but the silence grew too interminable to endure.

"Mathilda was born after you left." Ellen chatted nervously. "She's seven. Captain Papa died last year. There was a storm. Off the Carolinas. His schooner sank. The *Californian sank.*"

But of course Perk knew his schooner.

"No!" The pain in his voice felt like a mirror reflection of her heart. "Oh, El—that's awful news. I hadn't heard. Captain Prentiss is —that is, he was—such a great man. I'm so deeply sorry, Ellie."

"I should have been there when it happened," her heart said

back, hijacking her tongue. Her grief suddenly re-triggered by his sadness. "Sometimes, I wish I had been." Had she just said that out loud? "Oh, don't mind me. I've just missed—well, I've missed everything."

He nodded, and she realized that he was the one person alive who understood her well enough that she didn't need to clarify.

"I was always jealous that he was your father, you know," he admitted. "I think I've always wanted to be like him. To be *him*, really."

After a long pause, he finally looked up at her and tilted his head toward Salem. "You ever get out there? Since. I mean since—"

"Our trip?"

She thought of the wind, tugging her hair out of its lashings as they bounced along on their epic adventure. Perk steering, her navigating the currents and shoals, pulling up next to the merchantmen. The smell of tea and spices, cargo nets strung from the yards—the remnants of such exotic places. The dream they'd hatched to one day explore the world. Together.

Impossible, of course, but beautiful.

Who was she fooling with her mindless chatter? Perk knew every corner of her heart. All the keeping up of pretenses hit her as the most exhausting thing she'd ever done.

"A few times," she said, "But it was never the same. Our adventure was the best day of my life," she said. "And the worst. I was so wicked, Perk. I—"

She tried to say she was sorry, but sitting in her belly for eleven years, the stone of shame had grown too big to escape through her throat.

He grimaced suddenly, and she couldn't tell if it was from the rowing or the memory.

. . .

THEY FELL BACK to the uneasy silence. As they drew closer to the sand, she wondered whether to ask him about his family. Or his ship. Or his travels. She could barely imagine the life he must have led. But she felt she had no right to any of his stories.

Instead, she snuck glances at him as she talked to Mathilda. "You know you're in big trouble, right? You're going to have to apologize to Mr. Thompson for stealing his dory."

"Borrowing," Mathilda said. She seemed to come back to her precocious self, then, and began peppering Perk with questions.

"Where's your boat?" she asked.

"It's in New York," he said. "Docked on South Street."

Mathilda wouldn't understand what those words meant, but Ellen heard Perk's well-earned pride. The North River docks on the west side of Manhattan were for smaller coastal and rivercraft, while South Street was reserved for only the grandest of oceangoing vessels. Even the mighty *Californian* had only ever docked on the North River. That meant Perk had already achieved a grander commission than Captain Papa. A Caribbean run, maybe. Possibly, even one of the Atlantic packets to Liverpool.

"Is she big?" Mathilda continued.

"Not the largest merchantman in the fleet, I'm afraid." He chuckled. "But she's a full-rigged ship. Three sticks and fifteen squares."

A ship? Not a schooner or bark? Ellen was stunned. Mathilda looked up at her for an explanation and she tried not to show her surprise in case Perk read it as lack of confidence in his abilities.

"Three sticks means she carries three masts—fore, main, and mizzen. We've worked on your times tables. If each mast holds five square sails—three times five is?"

"Fifteen squares."

Perk whistled generously at her correct answer, and Ellen's heart swelled. Mathilda's teacher was trying to force her to memorize Bible passages instead.

"I hope you'll not think the less of me for her size, little Miss Prentiss," Perk said. "She's big enough to cross oceans at least."

. . .

ELLEN COULD SENSE this was a different Perk. A wiser one. There was a thoughtfulness in the way he chose his words. A sturdy confidence that had once been fleeting.

The bow thumped the sand, and Ellen felt a stab of disappointment instead of relief. Perk shipped the oars, stepping into the water gallantly to help the two ladies off.

Mathilda was cold but safe. Ellen was soaked but felt an inkling of herself again for the first time in months.

Perk extended his hand and when Ellen placed hers inside his, for one tiny instant, everything was alright again. Papa was alive. Perk was her best friend. The future was bright with possibilities.

Then, in the distance, she noticed a small crowd had gathered on the beach—Mrs. Dodge with her perpetually pursed lips, the pastor's wife, and several others whose faces blurred together in her anxiety. Of course, they'd witnessed the whole affair—again. In Marblehead, nothing stayed private for long.

It was uncannily like the day they'd come in from Salem. They'd been soaked then too, and nearly swamped, but had raced across the harbor with wild grins, dizzy with the victory of survival. Until they'd found everyone lined up on the beach, glaring with reproach. Mama'd nearly fainted. Mr. Creesy's face had been purple with rage.

But Ellen also felt a shade of the same victory, that thrill of doing something well. Of achieving a successful end.

Ellen helped Mathilda over the gunwale, acutely aware the whispers would already be starting. Poor girl. Would they now paint her with the same wild brush as they had Ellen? The girl shivered violently, her lips taking on a worrying bluish tinge.

"We need to get you home and into dry clothes," Ellen said, pulling her sister close.

Perk shielded her from the onlookers as he secured the second dory. As the 'faithless' groom, he must have felt the weight of their scorn even more than Ellen, but she was grateful for his broad shoulders.

"Do you sail to London?" Mathilda asked. The transition to land had no impact on her precocious interview, and Ellen secretly hoped she'd continue the questions all afternoon. As they began the walk from the sand to the street, she put a hand on Mathilda's shoulder to urge her to walk slower.

See what a good man looks like? Ellen wanted to tell her. Don't ever let yourself get pawned off to a cabbage farmer.

She wondered how to get Perk alone, in some quiet spot for her apology and also see to Mathilda. Should she invite him to dinner?

If she did, would he come?

"Been to London." Perk put his hands casually in his pockets as he walked. "Started on the packets as a cabin boy till I worked my way abaft the mast."

The details of Thames tidal charts swirled in Ellen's head, along with dreams she'd long tucked away. While she could recite the tables from memory, Perk had seen the real thing. Just as he'd lived all the adventures they'd once imagined together.

SHE MARVELED how once upon a time, he'd been awed by her visits to Boston and New York. She'd been the sailor, then. The traveler. The one with all the tales to tell. Now his world included England and the whole Atlantic, and she'd never been south of the eastern seaboard.

She watched him tie up the boats with practiced ease, his movements betraying years at sea. He'd grown a full head taller than her, but didn't stoop. He moved with the quiet assurance of someone who'd earned his place in the world.

Watching him now, she could see what others had always missed —the natural authority in his bearing, the careful way he gauged wind and water. He'd been born to command, regardless of what his father believed. Even as children, she'd recognized that spark of greatness in him, had seen how the sea called to something essential in his soul. Now that raw talent had been honed by experience, tempered like steel.

She feared he'd take the first opportunity on land to escape her company, but his fortitude had clearly grown along with his spine. He kept them company along the beach.

So much time had passed. And he acted with such grace. Perhaps he'd forgiven her after all. Maybe she didn't need to ruin things with an apology.

"But now I'm in the tea trade," he told Mathilda.

"China!" Only after Ellen spoke did she hear the unmitigated awe in her voice. A tea captain. The accomplishment made her gasp. It was the trade with the highest of financial stakes, the one that required the most exceptional navigational skills and seafaring experience in every condition. It was the most prestigious of all commands.

Even Mathilda had gone quiet in reverence as they walked along the half-moon of Great Neck Harbor.

"How is it?" Ellen asked.

"How's what?"

For a moment, she thought she'd spoken too much of what was in her heart. How is it to have such powerful hands? How does it feel to be free? But she'd spoken too little.

"How is it to spend your life at sea? Sailing the world?"

"Yes," he said.

"Yes?"

"Yes. It's all those things you imagine, El. Challenging and infuriating. Beautiful and vast. Full of terror and wonder. It's dynamic—always in motion, always in tension, always in transition. Well, you know. You've had a good taste of it."

"Hardly. My longest passage was four days. What was yours?"

Perk grimaced suddenly. "Too long."

Ellen couldn't understand the dark shift in his tone, but he seemed to recover himself and continued in a more pleasant manner.

"But yes, it is all those marvelous things and a lot more difficult ones as well. Relentless work, and cold, and damp for months on end. Violence ignited by the smallest slights when too many men are locked up in too small a space for too long. Never enough food or sleep."

He flashed her the wry grin that had always melted her heart. "It's the best life in the world." Then took three more steps before adding, "You'd adore it."

The old dreams flashed in front of her, dangerous as lightning. Sailing past the horizon. Seeing the Orient. The Pacific Islands. Exploring like Captain Cook.

"I'm up this way," Perk pointed with his thumb when they reached the fork between Darling and Front streets. "Will you be all right getting home from here?"

A polite goodbye, then. No dinner. No more time to be together. To talk. To explain.

"You've really done it," Ellen said, half stalling. "Everything we ever dreamed of."

Speaking the truth untwisted her insides as powerfully as strong drink. Then she heard her words and winced. "I mean you. That you dreamed of. I'm so proud of you, Perk."

Now he looked embarrassed.

"I'm sure you're the best captain in the fleet." Ellen spoke nervously now to cover her mistake, but her certainty was genuine.

"Wish I could agree," he said. "But I can't lie, Ellen."

Lie. The word stung like a slap. Had he meant for it to?

"I'm giving it everything I've got," he continued. "But I'm not doing so well."

Maybe he'd meant nothing by it.

"Just remember your currents, and you'll do fine," she said, remembering his incorrect angle to reach Mathilda. Ellen wrapped her sister in her coat again to buy a few more precious moments.

"I suppose I get too caught up in speed and lose sight of strategy," Perk said.

Self-awareness was a new quality. He'd matured, then.

"Oh, but you've always been a master of speed," she said. "It's your greatest strength. Don't sell yourself short. Trimming sail to get every quarter knot out, working the lifts and headers, steering straight as an arrow at the helm."

Mathilda wrestled to get out from under the coat. She was freezing. Ellen had to get her home.

"Would that speed was enough," Perk said. "Truth be told, I've been at the back of the fleet three seasons running. At this rate, there may not be a fourth."

He grew quiet, his face drawn, and for a moment, Ellen worried she'd overstepped the line again. But then he looked up. "Hey. Maybe you could teach me a navigation trick or two before I leave tomorrow morning."

"Tomorrow?" The word escaped before she could trap it behind her teeth. The shock of it stole her breath, her composure, everything she'd carefully constructed since seeing him again. Too soon. They'd barely begun to bridge the vast ocean of years between them.

He nodded but didn't explain. "I can't stay longer."

Tomorrow he'd vanish again, leaving her with nothing but memories and regret.

Can't stay.

Won't stay.

Won't stay for you.

A gust of wind cut through Ellen's damp clothes, sending a violent shiver through her that had nothing to do with the cold. Her fingers had gone numb, her skin prickled with gooseflesh, but she barely felt it. The physical discomfort paled against the ache of watching him prepare to leave again.

Even as she forced her feet to walk away, she couldn't take a breath. She kept waiting and waiting to suck in air that wouldn't come and wouldn't come. Until finally, it came in one great rush that almost knocked her over.

She turned and called back. "It'd take a lot longer than an afternoon to teach you proper navigation. You'll just to have to take me with you."

It was only when Perk shot her a look of terror that she realized what she'd said.

There was only one way a woman could travel with a man. He'd just squirmed out of one wedding. Did he think another would-be bride was throwing herself at him?

She nearly threw up her breakfast.

Perk swallowed, turning away from her before he spoke.

"Take care of yourself, Ellen," he said.

6

———————

Perk stepped through the Fountain Inn's narrow door, trying to release the deadened weight of January in favor of warm, yeasty air, full of spilled ale and hearty stew.

His worst fears had been realized by returning to Marblehead. Worse than his worst fears. Father's trap, Mother's near destitution, and now Ellen's—Ellen. He was soaked and exhausted from the row, but revived with an anger that vibrated from his jaw to his knuckles.

He'd almost been taken in by her confidence. By the ease with which they fell into working together. By their success at saving the plucky little girl.

He'd almost let himself forgive. Had humbled himself, even, to share his greatest fear. By God, had he'd even asked for her help! And her answer was so flippant, so impossible, so uncaring that it could only have been intended as ridicule.

You'll just have to take me with you.

It was time for a drink.

The fire's warmth pulled at his cold-stiffened muscles, and the slow, mournful notes of a fiddle matched his mood, but as he scanned the room, a dozen scowls bent in his direction, making it perfectly clear his presence was unwelcome.

Sod the lot of them.

He'd already posted two coppers on the worn bar—no chance the town scoundrel would be given credit today—when he saw Henry the Goat's broad frame at the far end.

His old friend startled at first, and Perk imagined him navigating loyalties, but he steadied quick enough.

"Well, if it isn't our very own captain," Henry called, crossing the room in three rolling strides. His calloused hand gripped Perk's with the strength of a sailor and steered him to a quiet table with a lamp. The chair had a wobbly leg that rocked as if Perk was still at sea.

He supposed, in a way, he was.

HENRY SET two mugs of ale on the table and took a seat opposite. Perk saw that his fingernails bore the gray-green marl of his father's trade, and the flickering oil flame revealed flecks of gray already entering his thick, black beard, but the creases at his eyes held the hint of amusement, not scorn.

"You've had a day of it," he said charitably.

He'd grown stocky since Perk had last seen him. Shoulders wide as a capstan now. Almost too big for the chair. Perk's muscles remembered Henry pinning him nine times out of ten, but measuring the mass of him now, he felt the odds had shifted toward a draw.

"You barely know the half of it," Perk said, trying to rub feeling back into his numb fingers. His hand drifted up to the stock at his neck, fingers fumbling with the buckle that felt like it was slowly strangling him. He was angry at himself for dressing in formal neck-wear, for dithering about the wedding until the very end. But he was furious with Ellen.

You'll just to have to take me with you.

Henry peered around his left shoulder, then his right, searching for prying ears, then spoke in a low voice. "Ask me, I'd say you just avoided shipwreck by the teeth of the tide, old friend."

The laugh caught Perk off guard, rising from somewhere deep in his belly. Even that small bark of breath loosened muscles he hadn't realized were coiled tight.

An old ship's wheel still hung on the wall above, its weathered spokes once gripped by a hundred helmsman. Perk had once held them himself in this very bar, when backs were safely turned, when sailing could live only in his imagination.

"Tell me about your life, Goat. Working the oyster beds by the look of it."

When Henry looked surprised, Perk pointed to his fingernails.

"Ah, yes. Well, not all of us can sail the ocean blue," he said.

"Not all of us had such reason to get away," Perk said, but his attempt at humor hit with a thud.

Henry nodded. Knew immediately what Perk meant. God, but it had been a lifetime since he'd felt the comfort of an old friend.

Blasted stock collar.

The starched linen had gone damp with sweat and was strangling him like a bloody octopus. Wretched thing. Never could manage the buckle without twisting his arms half out of joint. His fingers keep slipping off the brass. Might as well try to pick a lock behind his head.

Almost got it. Just need to—"Damn!" How did Father manage this noose every blessed day? No wonder he was always so sour-faced with his neck trapped in wire and horsehair like a personal pillory.

Henry held out his hand—a silent offer of help—but Perk stiffened at the thought of letting another man near his throat.

"No one's called me Goat in a good long while," Henry said, easing into a grin as Perk continued to struggle. "I believe I prefer it to Mr. Doyle. I still feel too young for that name. But I can't grumble about much. Make do well enough. The old skiff leaks something fierce, and my slicks are worn clean through. Lost Ma this last season —a mercy, truth be told, after all her suffering. Took up with Sarah

Winters. You remember her? Got myself two little girls now. That's about the whole of it."

He let out a chuckle. "Near forgot the Newfoundland. Smart as paint that little thing. There. My news in full. But Lord, Perk, you must have tales enough to fill a book."

It could have been a day that passed since Perk last saw him, not a decade. The ceramic mug sat cool against his palm as he drained half the ale, stomach tightening as he searched for the right words.

"Tell me about the ropewalk, first. Has Father's business foundered so deep that Bartlett is really the only lifeline?"

Henry's face twisted like he'd bitten into a rotten apple. "That explains the match, then. Wondered what might have bound you to that—" his eyes tracked the barman's glare, and he lifted his mug. "To the endlessly prim Miss Bartlett."

Perk's fingers slipped again on the buckle as sweat beaded down his neck, and he swallowed a curse.

Henry twisted his mug in a circle on the table, following the groove of many who'd done so before. "There are rumors of some hefty debts," he said. "Shares in a whale ship or two that met a bad end. But that's all I know of the ropewalk."

The windowpane shook from a gust of wind and Perk's shoulders sagged with the familiar weight of Father's follies. "That sounds like him. Always reaching for fool's gold when honest work sits an arm's length away. Remember when he got his hands on that load of cheap whalebone and was sure that weaving it into the hemp would keep the rope from freezing? Damn fool thought he was going to make a fortune. Instead, the fibers caught in every pulley."

Henry's chest shook with a harsh laugh. "Could I forget? The first time it got wet, the *Harriet*'s crew nearly mutinied over the stench of rotting blubber."

Perk wanted to mirror Henry's easy laugh, but couldn't forget he'd left Mother to wrestle with the failing business alone. That weight pressed against his chest with each breath, so he was determined to change the one thing he could, which was the state of his sobriety.

He reached again for the ale, seeking that familiar warmth that would unknot the tension coiled beneath his ribs.

After a long drink, he gave up trying to unbuckle the stock collar and threw Henry a nod of defeat. If he was already a dishonorable coward, he may as well be a man who could bend his pride enough to accept the help of an old friend.

"Tell me about your ship," Henry said, generously giving him room to crow as he unclasped the buckle.

The man who saw nothing but fair winds, Perk thought, whatever the surrounding weather. Just as he'd been as a boy.

Unfortunately today, even the mention of the *Oneida* sent a shudder through Perk that he tried to drown in the dregs of his ale.

"That bad? Are you done with the high seas already?" Henry asked.

The drink must already be running through Perk, he thought. Loosening his face. "No," he said. "Not that, anyway. It's the best thing I ever could have done. It's just—"

A shiver crawled up his spine, settling between his shoulder blades.

Henry kept his eyes fixed on his mug, giving Perk two arm's length of space across the table, and raised two fingers to the barkeep. His thoughtful patience felt like a warm blanket.

The simple path beckoned to Perk as he brushed the crusted salt from his beard with the back of his hand—make a quick jest, share an easy laugh. Then part ways and go change into dry clothes in the room above. Safe harbor.

But as the weak light pressed through the tavern's grimy windows —a curse of short winter days—something twisted in Perk's gut. That familiar knot of standing so alone. Not seeing a soul who knew the whole of him. Not one who'd touched his past. Felt its weight.

In his profession, even carefully selected friends were also rivals.

The rest were simply out for blood. Any errant word he spoke was sure to find its way back to Grinnell's spies. He barely remembered the warmth of honest friendship.

The ale sat heavy in his belly as he heard the words tumble out of his mouth.

"It's not bragging to tell you I was second to none as a sailor. Just honest. One of the greatest officers, even. But captain may have been a big step too far. I don't get what's wrong with me. Last season, the old man I used to sail for, Captain Howland, gave me a pretty stark warning. This year, the talk came from Mr. Grinnell himself."

Each confession dropped like a sounding lead.

"Look," Perk said, tracing a path across the water stains on the table. "I can feel when the ship wants to run. Know exactly how much canvas she can take. Then we hit the Cape, and I swear it's like trying to walk up a waterfall. And yet, Palmer, Waterman, Low—all of them—thrashed me so soundly it was like they'd found a secret shortcut through the middle of Africa.

"And don't get me started on the damned sights that never add up right. Old Man Howland used to just glance at the tables and know exactly where he was. Me? I'd have better luck reading tea leaves. It takes hours to work through all the trigonometry of a celestial sight, and even then, I'm always waiting for old Mr. Whittaker to rap my knuckles with the ferule."

Henry's easy laugh gave Perk a nudge of courage and he took another pull of ale, pride burning worse than the drink.

"Never told a soul this before, but I lost four days backtracking near Sumatra last season because of a calculation error. I'm just lucky my mate's more hopeless at navigation than I am and didn't notice. Sometimes it's so bad, I even wish I'd been born a Brit."

When Henry gave a puzzled squint, Perk explained. "London tea prices are fixed, so speed to market's irrelevant. Their ships don't race home, they dodder. Reef the sails every bloody sunset, like a bunch of old men."

"You wouldn't have lasted ten minutes as a British tea captain," Henry laughed. "You're a born competitor, Perk."

He had to give him that point. "Maybe," Perk answered, "But I've only got half the constitution for the job. The truth of it is, only three years in, and my command's already in jeopardy."

Then he realized he'd boxed himself in. Had to finish the full, messy job of the distasteful confession. "I can sail swift enough for the front of the fleet, but if I don't sail in the fastest direction—" his head hurt just thinking about it. "If I had a good chart man for a mate, I could take every bleeding one of 'em. But I got stuck with Grinnell's cousin instead—more parlor pet than sailor. Wears pearl buttons for Chrissakes. An empty hat, just there because of his name."

"I've found the sea's rather indifferent to one's ancestry," Henry said with a wry smile.

Perk had expected to stop there, but Henry was working out the bitterness of the day, and the drink was doing its job to boot. So he told him the rest. About the dory. About Mathilda. And then—even Ellen's ludicrous proposal.

"Can you imagine?" Perk swept his arms wide, ale splashing on the floor. "On the last wobbly leg of my command? What they'd say if I brought on a woman to set my courses?"

Henry stopped smiling.

"What?" Perk asked, after a silence.

Henry hesitated.

"You're not taking her seriously? There's never been—"

"—Don't know if I am, or I'm not, Perk—"

"—a woman navigator in the entire history of seafaring—"

"—I get you're in a tough spot, and I'm just a humble oysterman—"

"—the last thing I need is another reason for their contempt—"

"—Just hear me out, will you, goddammit?"

Henry's mug struck the table with enough force that Perk's throat closed up mid-sentence. The pressure behind his eyes built like an approaching storm, and his shoulders tensed at the thought of another Father-like speech. But he told himself this was Henry.

Unlike Father, Henry's advice had always been true.

"I know nothing of that high-stakes world of yours," he said. "Tea chests and Chinamen and the Upper Tens of the blasted city. You've seen things I'll never even dream of, and I'm sure there's smarter folk you could ask. But I'll share the little I do know."

He pointed toward the harbor with his thumb. "Most folks look out there and they see waves. Somehow, I see the oyster beds underneath 'em. I can't explain how—something about the way the currents move, the colors shift, the way the foam gathers on the water. I'll wager it's like that for you with the wind and your ship. You see things invisible to most, don't you? I bet you're shaping a sail before you've even realized the wind's changed. Am I right?"

Perk had to nod, but he did so warily.

"You know well as I do that Ellen's always been that way with numbers. Like a second sight. Can see what's invisible to you'n me. Remember when she told your father he'd miscalculated the cordage required for the stays on Cap Prentiss's schooner?"

"Caught him in a lie, you mean? Trying to double his sale?" Perk remembered. She was nine years old. Standing up to Father in a way he still couldn't. "Are you saying—"

"I'm not saying anything apart from what looks plain enough to me. Over here, I have a friend who'll lose his beloved career without a good navigator. And over there, I have a friend who's a brilliant navigator—"

"—I'd be a laughingstock from South Street to Whampoa—"

"—I doubt folk would understand at the start—"

"—putting it mildly—"

"But what about when you win?"

. . .

He stopped Perk cold with that one. Unbidden, the vision of being the first man of the season to slide into Dock 19 crept into his mind, quiet as a fog.

"You're a man of instincts," Henry said. "Always have been. What do they tell you now?"

He could win.

He knew that as clearly as Henry knew his oyster beds.

His gut tightened at the thought. It wasn't unheard of for captains to sail with their wives. Even Old Man Howland had done it, and the ridicule had mostly fallen away after he'd outrun Palmer in '36.

But there was so much more Perk couldn't put into words for Henry. Mrs. Howland had ironed her husband's shirts, minded their children, and occasionally baked a pie for the officers. She hadn't stood on the quarterdeck taking sun sights in front of twenty-two crewmen.

More importantly, Mrs. Howland bent-to like any sailor when the captain spoke.

Ellen? The muscles in Perk's jaw tightened. Ellen wouldn't mind a rule unless it minded her first.

A captain's authority lived in the eyes of his crew. One sideways glance, one moment of hesitation, and the whole careful balance could unravel like a poorly spliced rope.

Just last season, Captain Moore had lost the *Artemis* because his mate had talked back and not been whipped for it. Within two hours, the crew had started dragging their feet at every order. Within two days, his commands were openly questioned. Moore had been lucky to reach New York without a full-on mutiny, but would never be employed aboard a ship again, either afore or abaft the mast.

Meanwhile, Ellen was as trustworthy as a card sharp.

Perk shook his head firmly, and saw Henry's shoulders drop.

"Too bad," his friend said, watching a mouse test the air near the bar's foot rail. "It's not on you to save her, though. I appreciate—"

"What do you mean, save?"

The fiddle fell silent. The tavern air grew still as slack water, leaving only the steady tap of the icicle melting against the sill.

"I don't want to add to your burden, Perk," Henry said carefully, quieter without the music to hide their conversation. "It's just—I know what she meant to you once."

Perk's jaw clenched tight enough to crack a walnut. "What are you not telling me?"

Henry sighed. "It's like she's only half alive these days, and fading more each time I see her. You know she was only supposed to miss the one voyage of the *Californian,* to look after Mathilda when her mother took ill. Then word came last summer that the schooner'd been lost and Ellen lost her father, her prospects, and the family's income all in one go."

Perk's fingers traced the worn grain of the table. Anything to keep him from thinking about the past.

"Now it's like she's forgotten how to breathe," Henry added quietly. "And then for Bartlett to turn on her today—"

"—What did that pompous windbag do this time?"

"Near as not preached a whole sermon about the evils of Ellen Prentiss," Henry said. "I doubt she'll see so much as a kind nod in this town any sooner than you will. And not that you're asking, but yes, I'm sure the two are related. Bartlett must have blamed her for his daughter's disappointment."

The muscles in Perk's shoulders pulled tight. "But that's ludicrous! Ellen had nothing to do with me refusing to marry a self-righteous blue cow!"

Henry threw Perk a withering glare and indicated the many ears that were listening. Was he speaking too loud? He could barely notice anymore.

He was too furious. He'd been prepared for his decision to ruin his own reputation in Marblehead. He'd never thought it would touch Ellen's. That made no sense.

But his guilt only ran so far.

"Are you saying that I should seriously consider—you realize you're talking about marriage, Goat. A lifetime commitment. To *Ellen*, of all people. You know what she did to me."

Henry shrugged his shoulders. "I'd never suggest a thing to a man who knows his business. I'd only ask: what if someone took the sea away from *you*?"

"They tried," Perk snarled, shoulders tensing against the weight of the words, forcing away the shame of how he'd just burned down his mother's world to save his connection to the sea. The ale's warmth beckoned, promising to blur the sharp edges of the conversation. He finished the glass and gestured to the barkeep for a whiskey to replace it.

For an unintentional heartbeat, he imagined the steadiness of Ellen with him at sea, a friend to brace against a storm. A head for numbers. 'Quick as a compass and twice as reliable,' Captain Prentiss always used to say about her. A hearty soul who could weather the rough seas of his tempers and steady his mind, the way Henry was now.

But there was the keel-destroying reef, right there.

Two points to starboard.

It didn't matter how much his gut churned at the thought of losing his ship, or how his chest swelled with the desire to crush Father with his success.

He couldn't paper over the critical fact that aboard his ship, Henry would have obeyed an order, while Ellen still acted like his master.

"It's impossible." The words slipped out, barely stirring the air.

Henry nodded. Kept his distance. "I'm sure you'll figure it out, Perk," he said. His voice sounded farther off, like a ship's bell in fog. He drained his glass. "I'd best be getting home."

He rose, turned to the window as if searching for words, then dropped back into his chair.

"Best steady yourself," he said. "Your father's on his way in."

––––––

Perk had hoped to slink out of town before the bastard learned where he was staying, but it was always going to be a long shot. The door crashed open, and Father surged through like a whirlwind.

"You," he spat.

Perk pushed back his chair as he stood. Defensive move. If there'd been a back door, he would have been through it, but he was cornered, forced to stare the old man down.

"You didn't leave me much choice," he said.

"—Ungrateful bastard. Shaming the family so publicly. Always thinking yourself so superior to your old man—"

That surprised like a slap.

"Superior? When you work behind my back to choose for me a sanctimonious parlor ornament for a wife? Someone who'd never dare think for herself?"

"This was never about Miss Bartlett, and we both know it. I heard where you were this morning!"

The ale made Perk's thoughts pitch and roll in confusion. This morning he'd been at the inn. He'd been walking along the shore.

"You were with that Prentiss harlot again!" Father's words struck him like a physical blow. "Same one who ruined your life the first time, making you run off to sea."

Perk recalled the reasons he'd run off to sea. They included the back of Father's hand. The crack of his fist. The leather of his belt. His fists ached from how tight he was squeezing them.

"Her sister needed help. What does any of that—"

"Didn't I always say there was something unnatural about that girl? Had the mark of the devil 'fore she was six years old, that one. Running wild. Climbing trees. You were always so blind to her spells, and now you let her trick you out of a perfectly good match—"

"She had nothing to do with—" But the words caught like an anchor in his throat. He reached inside, feeling for the jagged edge that held them back, needing to clear her name of the one charge she was actually innocent of.

You'll just have to take me with you.

"—spurn a good woman like Miss Bartlett for one who's indecent. Competitive. Goddamn ambitious. Always pushing into men's business!"

Perk's gut tightened at memories of his mother bent over the kitchen table—pencil in one hand, spoon in the other—her shoulders curved against the weight of father's debts. Her fingers secretly scratching out letters under father's name to save the firm from sinking.

"And what's to say some women aren't better at men's business than men are?" His fists coiled and he bent his weight forward until he could feel Father's breath on his face. "Maybe some men would be better off if they weren't so threatened by a mere woman that they could see how valuable it was to actually invite her into their business."

"You've gone soft in that salt air," Father shot back. "What kind of man would debase himself enough to rely on a woman's help?"

You! Perk wanted to yell. You'd have spent the last two decades in debtors' prison if it wasn't for your wife! His lungs screamed to shout the words, but the memory of Mother's bruises anchored his tongue.

Instead, he let loose the words he knew would cut next deepest:

"Your son!"

7

The steps came as naturally to Ellen as breathing.

First: find Ursa Major. It was too dark to see the harbor out the study window, and almost fully overcast. Yet between the stretches of black sky where the stars remained hidden by clouds, there was a clearing. She found the Big Dipper right where she'd expected it. The constellation had migrated from low in the north-northeast to mid-sky in the northwest, which meant the deepest stretch of night had descended like a hollow ache.

Second: follow the leading dots of its bowl, Dubhe and Merak, as they pointed toward her old friend the North Star. And there he was, winking at her in the night, as if nothing at all had changed.

As if she hadn't been seared by loss. Again.

Third: stand steady, train the sextant's eyepiece on Polaris, and draw him down to the horizon with the mirror dials, measuring the angle.

She didn't have a sextant, of course. It had been lost with the *Californian*, but she dug into Captain Papa's mahogany desk until she unearthed his old spyglass instead.

The cool brass against her eyebrow almost approximated her

favorite instrument, but the spyglass itself was too light and too long to hold stable in the normal manner, with her elbows pulled into her chest. She had to extend her right arm to keep the end from wobbling.

She was able to capture Polaris in its lens, but that brought another problem. Instead of a pinpoint of light she was used to seeing, the image leapt back at her at twenty-times magnification—as a sickly, jaundiced eye.

Way too close. Too menacing.

She'd tried to re-create that fleeting sense of her power, but as she set down the spyglass she chastised herself for indulging in such sentimentality. Her life at sea was as well and truly over, and the time had come to—

BAM!

The sound made her jump, and she couldn't immediately place it. Had a bird hit the roof?

BAM! BAM! BAM!

The front door.

In the middle of the night? Muffled pounding against the wood. Fists, not knuckles. Bottom drawer on the right. Papa's flintlock.

She grabbed it and flew down the stairs hoping the sight of the weapon might be enough to deter an intruder, as it offered little protection. They had neither powder nor shot in the house.

"Stay upstairs!" She yelled to Mathilda and Mama.

In the salon, she crept toward the door, then crouched into a protective stance. Her bare feet soaked up the cold but provided better balance than slippers. She gripped the pistol in her left hand, then reached out with her right to grasp the handle.

She took one last second to calculate a plan of attack.

One: shock the intruder with the leveled pistol. Two: land an overhead blow, flintlock to skull. Three: use the door itself as a weapon. Four: if conditions required, shout for neighbors.

She flung the door open.

Even in the darkness, Perk's massive form was easily recognizable.

So was the overpowering smell of whiskey.

"Don't shoot," he said, holding up both hands automatically. Then he wobbled and grabbed the banister for support. "Though if you must, aim for my pride at least."

Ellen lowered the weapon.

"What are you doing here?" she hissed.

"Good question. What the goddamn hell am I doing?" His voice rose as if he was asking the stars themselves—at a drunken man's volume—scandalizing all of Front Street with his loud swearing in the dead of night.

He paused long enough that Ellen thought he'd finished, but then started right up again. "I had a beginning. That is to say, Miss Prentiss—"

That startled her almost as much as the knock itself.

Miss Prentiss?

"I had a speech. Planned on the walk over, but the words, the words keep jumbling around. Like the blasted numbers do."

Was he slurring? He stood bareheaded on the porch, cap cradled in his left arm.

She was wearing only her shift and tugged at the shawl to make sure it covered everything that needed covering. When had she last brushed her hair? She set the pistol on the hall table.

"Do you know what time—"

"Oh!" he said. "Your sister. Little slip of a girl. Magnificent fighter. Like you to the button. Is she—"

"She's fine," Ellen whispered, trying to cue him that the whole street could hear his every word as it sliced the quiet air.

He didn't take the hint.

"—I've just had the most brilliant idea. After six glasses of . . . brilliant ideas. Maybe eight."

He glanced about, and finding nowhere suitable to set his cap, laid it purposefully on her head. He straightened it there, then straightened it again.

A trace of his warmth lingered against her scalp.

"Blast that cunt of a Goat!" he said suddenly. "This is a hell of a lot harder than he said it would be."

Perk was off his head.

"Perhaps you should come inside."

"A captain can bring his wife. You know. Aboard."

He'd caved and married Euphemia after all, Ellen realized. Her heart grew spiky thorns. "I know a captain's privileges," she said. "You needn't beat on my door—"

"I can drive a boat like a man possessed," he said. "Like the very devil's on our heels. But not when I have to spend half the day floundering in sums, and the rest of it hunting for winds that never come—"

"—You want me to teach that lackwit how to navigate for you?" Her thorns grew thorns. "She wouldn't know a line of position if it stepped on her toe!"

"What's a lackwit? Piss and biscuits, Ellen. What are you on about?"

"I'm sure you and Miss Bartlett will be very happy together."

"That's not—" His left hand, tugged at his curls just like when he used to sit perplexed at his slate.

"I'm grateful for your help today," she said. "That is yesterday, I suppose, seeing it's *nearly dawn*. But it's the middle of the night and—"

Suddenly, he grabbed her hands and closed his palms around them like a clam shell. His fingers were colder than hers, but his touch—

"You'd have to obey me," he said.

That left her speechless for a full minute. "I'd have to what?"

"You're so bloody smart. And brave. And full of fire," he said, his calloused palms pressed against the back of her fingers. "Why is everyone else so dead? Prim." He pursed his lips and drew his shoulders in as tight as they'd go. "I hate prim. Would you like another dash of tea, Mr. Creesy?"

His voice held a tone of mockery and—oddly—a British accent. Then he nearly lost his footing, and Ellen had to brace her shoulder against his to keep him steady, but he kept talking as if he hadn't noticed.

"And you're a navigator. Good God. If only you weren't so— Ellen."

Unlike Perk, she was well aware that the neighbors were gripping the bedclothes, leaning toward windows, trying to catch every word. She was tempted to shout at him but wrenched her hands away instead. The variables of his jumbled statements kept trying to form themselves into a solvable equation.

Captain + Wife + Navigator = Euphemia?

Captain + Euphemia = Navigator + Wife?

Captain = Navigator / Wife?

"And what exactly does it mean to be Ellen?"

His eyes found hers. Dark as it was, she could see they were wide, wet. Scared, even.

"She's a converted packet," he said, ignoring her question. "A 750 tonner. Beamier than a plough horse and prone to wallow in a seaway, but stout enough. Mate's a gentrified jackass but the crew are all solid Swedes and Finns."

He was talking in circles, but she felt a rush of warmth that he'd paid her the compliment of knowing the seafaring world. Behind the puzzle of his words, some sense was beginning to form. Scandinavians were professional, oceangoing crew. Not like the Liverpool packet thugs.

"I'm glad for you, Perk," she said carefully, heart hammering in her chest. "What is it—exactly—you're trying to say?"

"I can't lose my command. Can't live without the sea." He looked up, as if wondering if he needed to give more detail. "Run the tea route with me?"

The answer clicked into place like the last tumblers of a lock.

Navigator = Wife

HER HEART LURCHED into her throat. Perk's drunken stumbling was a proposal.

She could have her life back. Better! Whole oceans. And the tea trade. Following the monsoons. All the seas she'd charted but never sailed. Long dormant hope, that most dangerous of creatures, unfurled its sails. But there were other pieces of his puzzling declarations that tugged at her emotions with a contrary tide.

You'd have to obey me.

That damnable word, *obey*, sat like grit in an oyster. Ellen forced herself to breathe, to think beyond the wild pulse hammering at her temples. Perk swayed before her, his eyes pleading for understanding she wasn't sure she could give.

"You're asking me—" Her voice caught, strange and thin. She steadied it with effort. "—to navigate your ship to China." The collision of two realities so impossible, she had to whisper it. "As your *wife?*"

"Aye," he said. "You've caught it there." He seemed to want to say more before reconsidering it. Letting a nod take the place of any further explanation.

She could practically feel the solidity of a mizzen mast against her back. The heft of a sextant in her hands again, the entire basket of stars above her. The freedom to be her truest self. To act from the dictates of her own mind. To feel, once again, her power in commanding the very heavens.

She bit the smile from her lip.

She had to think this through. Had to be practical. She knew a different version of Perk, a reflection of the past. Not who he'd become.

Who was he now? A drunken man at her door proposing to take her to sea.

He stared at her face, almost curiously. Then surprised her by laying his finger on her nose, as if to explore it. He was gentle, but his hands were ice cold.

"We get tugged out Tuesday on the morning tide."

Her head swam. His face so close to hers. Head tilted, looking straight at her. Almost through her.

She forced the tide tables into her mind to stop the swirl of feelings. Tuesday morning's ebb began at 7:18 here in Marblehead. New York must be three or four hours later down there. At 10:30 or 11, maybe? His ship was in New York and today was Sunday. No, Monday morning. The overnight steamer would barely arrive in time.

"You left things a bit late," she said, gently.

"Wasn't going to come home," he said. "Until I did."

His finger slipped from her nose and traced a path, slowly, meditatively, around her lips. Then he took both his hands back.

"Ellen—" he said, as if the word itself sobered him up. "I mean it. You'd have to obey me. Could you do that? You'd have to make a solemn vow. Otherwise, it's impossible."

"Vow?" Her voice squeaked from a dry throat. The resurrected feeling of power faded into dust.

"To respect the natural order of—"

"The natural order?" She stepped back.

Had he become a Bartlett disciple after all this time?

A woman's sole task on this earth is to obey!

"Rightful authority, anyway," he said.

His words ripped the wool of feelings and desires from her eyes.

Oh, foolish, foolish hope! Now she could see his proposal for what it was. Not love, certainly. Not even partnership. Merely desperation.

He didn't offer her freedom. Merely another type of prison. One as invisible as it was inescapable. A lifetime of living inside Bartlett's rules.

"No."

Dashed hopes and grief and guilt and fear pressed into the backs of her eyeballs. Tears threatened.

"While I appreciate your offer, Perk, I'm afraid I could never—" She struggled to speak. Pain had twisted her words until even her voice sounded different.

"—merely mean that one's wife must yield to—"

Choked sobs would soon follow and Perk would be able to see the worst kind of ugliness leaking out of her. She'd rather throw herself into the sea than allow that.

"Absolutely not, Captain Creesy!"

She slammed the door just in time to hide behind it as the flood of tears swept her to the ground.

8

"Good riddance!"

A man with a handcart spun around and threw Perk a hard stare.

"Pardon," he said, reflexively tipping his cap. Then he grew furious with himself. *What are you apologizing for, you squid?*

The fury felt good, felt right.

Are you captain of the fucking Oneida *or a sniveling, lovesick schoolboy? You just skirted disaster. Thank providence and get the hell out of here while you still can, Perk.*

He carved a path between two men digging a posthole, but was still too far from the gangplank to avoid the glares of every fisherman and dock worker on the wharf. Or their laughter.

He imagined their jokes. The prodigal son returns, riddled with pride, only to fail at two marriages in a single day.

That must be some kind of record, Perk thought bitterly. Likely the only one he'd ever earn: The Greatest Buffoon in all of History.

. . .

WITH EVERY STEP, his skull throbbed like the blue devils. Mr. Mills was the only one who caught Perk's eye, his old face soft with understanding—worse somehow than the mockery.

Perk's spine stiffened. He didn't need his pity or anyone else's.

Even Ellen had mocked him. She'd seen right through his polished buttons to how much of a pathetic, muttonheaded, milksop he actually was.

His teeth ached from clenching his jaw so tight.

No one on earth knew him better than she did, and her judgement had been the harshest—and most accurate—of all.

Even she didn't trust him to be her captain.

The steamer waited at the dock, the acidic bite of its coal dust scratching at his throat. At a camp table set up on the landing, a company agent checked Perk's name in his ledger book.

"Berth sixteen," he said, winking at the deckhand—a boy of twelve or thirteen—who couldn't contain his amused grin.

Even the bloody ferry crew had heard of his humiliation. Six to one, the news would make it to the *Oneida*'s crew before he could depart tomorrow. Better odds yet that Grinnell would hear of it soon after. Perfect excuse to send him on some shit-packer voyage to a guano island in South America.

That ungrateful—

OH, but she'd done him a favor, really. Fool that he was. Drunk and stupid, trying to skirt the impossible problem. Far more serious, even, than the demeaning jokes and career-ending ridicule he would have faced for giving a wife an officer's role.

He'd let Henry talk him into a ridiculous notion. Henry, who sailed his dory alone. Who only knew the wet of the sea—the constant damp of clothing, fingers too numb to unbuckle a belt, feet turned to ice blocks.

He didn't know the bone-dry resentments that grew beneath that sodden surface on a long voyage. How it was with men—even good men—when you took away sleep, sex, food, and a dry pair of drawers. When you risked their lives with every sail change, and forced them to live cheek by jowl for month after unbroken month.

How harmless banter got misinterpreted. How quickly trivial disputes festered into savage vendettas. Quibbles became rivalries that grew into blood feuds such that one petty slight could flare to a blazing fight in seconds.

Crew conflicts were the true cause of too many disasters at sea. Too many mutinies. Not in the official records, of course, but in the ale houses where tongues loosened with drink spoke the truth.

Perk had seen the deadly consequences himself. Men too busy quarreling to notice approaching dangers.

He sometimes felt like it wasn't so much a ship he sailed as a floating powder keg.

The only way to keep that swirling mess of men in check was to ensure the command structure was absolutely inviolate. Orders given must be orders followed. When their watch bell rang, they damn well stood their watch. If they were sent to reef the mizzen topsail, they'd better be halfway up the ratlines before they gave a second thought to the icicles hanging from the rigging. And the captain—lynchpin of the whole order—must be obeyed without hesitation. Without debate.

Without bloody question.

To have thrown Ellen in the mix would have been to introduce a lit match.

Absolutely not, Captain Creesy!

His rage flared, then ebbed, leaving something colder in its wake. Three strides across the gangway, his fingers grew tight around the sea bag's strap as if it might anchor him to some kind of dignity.

The dining saloon had a fire going, but he craved solitude. He longed for the scratchy pillow and hard bunk, even the chuffing of the boiler on the other side of the wall, to drown out the sound of his own thoughts.

Also possibly, depending on how the day went, to vomit.

He passed a half-dozen doors until he came to his cabin, where he was surprised to find the door open.

He was even more surprised to find Patience inside.

She was leaning back on the narrow bunk built into the wall, shivering in a coat too small to summit her mountain of a belly. The moment she tried to lever herself up, he felt the strain in his own spine.

"Take my coat for Chrissakes," Perk said. "What are you doing here? You'll catch your death."

A dozen concerns struck him at once.

"Are you running away from the boot maker? What did Pierce do to you? I'll kill him—"

"—Will you shut that blather box of yours and help me up?"

Perk had never served on a whaler, but he imagined the sweaty maneuvers required to bring his very pregnant sister up to a sitting position would have been familiar to one who had.

The cabin was barely a fathom across, mostly a bunk and a wash basin, but there was a child-size chair in the corner. He folded himself into it.

"Now then. I'm here to see you off because Father forbade it of Mother."

A sharp knock echoed from somewhere down the walkway. A key perhaps, against a solid wood door. "All visitors to depart now," shouted a far-off voice.

"I couldn't have worked for Father," Perk said. "It would have been the death of me."

"Of course you couldn't. Plus, you worked half your life to get that command. You made the right decision, Perk."

If only that were enough to assuage his guilt. "I promise you I'll find a way to get her money." He sat rigid in the tiny chair, jaw clenched.

"Money?" She folded her arms atop her hump like it was a built-in shelf.

"I heard Father might lose the ropewalk," he said. Goat rarely got things wrong. "Was I misinformed?"

"Hardly," she said, dashing his fragile hope. "Father's all but lost it already. He's as dumb as he is deaf if he ever thought an investment from Bartlett would change that."

Her dark curls, he realized, were the exact color of his own. Now that she was here in front of him, he missed his sister more than he had in the entirety of his time at sea.

"I swear I won't leave her destitute," he said. "I just need one more season."

"She doesn't need your money, Perk."

Now she was talking nonsense. No ropewalk, no income. Riled up as he was, he realized he should soften his tone. The pregnancy was obviously making her soft in the head.

Patience leaned forward—no minor effort, that—and whispered. "She's Mother. Don't you think she's seen this coming for years? Same as she did the panic of '37? Tell me. Who does the cordage company books?"

"Mother, but—"

"And who secures the revenue at the bank?"

"Mother, of course, but it's Father's name on the account. Even if there were funds, she'd have no control over them. And if he's got debts, the collectors'll wipe that ledger clean."

She nodded, scrunched up her nose, and for a second he glimpsed the playful seven-year-old Patience. "And who's smart enough to know exactly the same things you so astutely pointed out?"

Prickles broke out on his scalp. "Mother."

"Mother," she agreed. "She was just grateful to see you one last time before she disappears. Come spring, when—"

"What?"

His head was spinning enough he grasped the edge of the wash basin, just in case he couldn't hold back the contents of his stomach.

"Will you just listen? I know you're used to giving the commands, big brother, but today, for all that's holy, I'm ordering you to shut it. We have little time. The next time Father goes to Boston, our very capable mother will pack her bag and take this very steamer to New York, where she'll board a sailing ship to Louisiana as the Widow Sinclair. When she arrives, she'll take over as the sole agent of P&P Cordage in New Orleans."

This was getting as convoluted as his disastrous discussion with Ellen, and he was just as lost. "I don't understand. Who's given Mother a job?"

"All visitors to disembark!" The shout came from the other side of the door.

"The officially registered, absentee owner of the business is a certain Mr. Daniel Pierce of Marblehead, Massachusetts."

Pierce. The boot maker? Perk pulled at his hair, as if he could straighten her words into tidy sense so easily. "What does your husband know of a ropewalk?"

Patience sighed and shook her head. "Oh my dearest, densest brother. Danny knows nothing about rope. Has no interest in it whatsoever. He's happy as a barnacle making boots and gloves. Sea boots. Riding boots. Button boots. Brogans. If it holds a hand or a foot, that man's pleased enough to shape it. But he does have an interest in me —and thus in Mother. Do you see now?"

He fell back into the chair so hard he nearly broke it.

Patience winked. "Between you, me, and the *Essex Maid*," she said, "My darling husband let her use his name for the paperwork. But it's her business."

His throat closed like a fist around the words, his chest expanding nearly past what his ribs could contain. He had to turn away. To fight both tears and a smile at the same time.

"Mother owns her own ropewalk?" His voice came out as a squeak.

"Now there's the Perkins I'm familiar with," she said, a smile evident in the pitch of her voice. "You're harder on yourself than Father ever was, but you're wiser than you know."

He still couldn't look at her. Studied the peg on the wall as if his life depended on knowing every detail. Unpainted. Rounded end. Too short to hang a hat.

Mother would be okay. She'd charted her own course through waters he'd thought unnavigable and would soon have all of New Orleans in her palm.

Was that Ellen's aim too? Something to call her own? He'd swear there'd been a glow in her eyes for a moment before it all went to hell. Hadn't there? He wished to hell he'd been sober enough to remember clearly.

Finally, he wrestled back control of himself. "Well, I'm right sorry I can't thank Daniel Pierce in person," he said. "Tell you what, though. In return for his kindness, I give him use of my name for the babe. How 'bout that? Don't you think another Perkins would improve the overall handsomeness of the world?"

She snorted. "And if it's a girl?"

"Well, the same, of course."

She held her lips tight, but her cheeks gave away her smile. She blinked a few times, wrestling with her own control of her face. "You know—"

A DEEP AND resonant BLAAAAAT sounded as if it came from the other side of the wall, from behind the door, from the inside of his head, simultaneously.

When it finished, Patience laughed outright, shook her head, and then fixed Perk with both of her loving eyes. "Time for me to waddle back to my world," she said. "And you to head toward yours. Help me to the gangplank?"

A minute ago, all he'd wanted was solitude. Now it crushed him to see her off. But he stood and helped her up, tried to show he could follow orders as well as give them.

He was even kind enough not to tell her she was heavier than a lumper on a drunk.

Her gloved hand traced the rail even as her steps hesitated. Sturdy leather, sheepskin lined. Daniel Pierce did good work.

"Euphemia would have given you a lifetime of misery," she finally said. She slowed her pace as they neared the gate and gazed out over the wharves, nodding at a fisher wife on the quay before turning back to him. "But don't give up on marriage just yet, Perk."

He slipped on the icy deck and nearly bit his tongue in half.

"Oh, of course I heard of your midnight ramblings. There isn't a soul in Marblehead outside the graveyard who hasn't."

"What a relief," he said, trying to sound convincing. "May I ask you then to extend to Ellen my everlasting gratitude for refusing such a ridiculous notion."

"Don't be glib, brother. You're hurting and I can see it plain as day." Her eyes anchored on Perk's like she was taking a depth sounding, measuring fathoms he couldn't hide.

He tasted iron. Swallowed blood.

"You know a lot of things I don't," she said. "But I know some too. The right partner can make you—I don't know how to say it, exactly, but better. Better than you already are. Better than you even knew you could be."

He steadied her descent down the gangplank with his arm, each step a careful negotiation between her shifting center of gravity and the ice-slick wood.

He suddenly wanted his solitude back like he wanted air to breathe.

"A life at sea hasn't changed that heart of yours, brother—no matter how much you try to hide it."

The weight of her gaze pressed against his chest, demanding something he couldn't name.

"The only thing ridiculous about your proposal was the hour in which you chose to deliver it. Well, that and being sotted. But don't give up on Ellen. Being tenderhearted enough to love someone is the hardest thing you'll ever do, Perk. Harder than crossing oceans or braving storms."

She pounded him once in the chest with her fist for emphasis.

"It's also the only thing in the world that truly matters."

9

———————

The slamming door reverberated through the dead of night, rattling the house, and echoing through Ellen's head.

She sat sprawled on the floor, back against the door, shaking. What a perfect fool Perk had just made of her.

Her eyes grew wet.

"Ellen?"

His voice through the door. She didn't answer.

From the other side came a thud, then a loud creak. The railing, perhaps? Another thud was certainly the sound of Perk stumbling down the porch stairs.

And then—silence.

A single tear escaped Ellen's left eye, tracing a hot, wet line down her cheek.

She'd not let another follow.

She stood and paced the salon—four steps, four steps, four steps. The space was too tight to vent her fury, yet it was still too dark to venture outside and unleash her wrath on the shore.

Another tear threatened. She slapped her cheek to startle it into submission. The hollow ache of loss had become familiar, but this new ball of searing pain would devour her if she let it.

The floorboards creaked loudly above. Too heavy to be Mathilda.

"Mama," Ellen said, barely holding herself together. "I don't want to hear it. Not now." Her voice vibrated with emotion.

"Dearest—"

"Not now! Leave me alone! Please!" she shouted. The neighbors could probably hear that too.

There was a pause, and then Mama said, "As you wish. We'll talk in the morning. But please know my dear that it'll be okay."

The creaks retreated in the direction of Mama's bedroom.

Perk wasn't Captain Papa. He didn't want a professional navigator. He didn't even want a partner.

You'd have to obey me.

He wanted a subordinate. A subservient helpmeet. A minion.

Four steps. Four steps. Four steps.

She crossed to the fireplace, ran her hand over the mantle until she found the flint—cool and smooth between her fingers on the flat side.

Perk tugging at his curls.

She drew the stone into her right palm, gripping its irregular, sharp edges until they drew just the right amount of raw pain.

Hold.

Hurt.

Finally, she opened the worn tinder box with her other hand and felt for the papery texture of dried fungus inside. It was primed, so she took up the steel striker.

Holding both hands near the box, she struck hard, flint against steel, producing a harsh clack. The wrong sound for control. Too much force, too wide a striking angle. A wild shower of orange-yellow sparks arced through the air like shooting stars, briefly illuminating her hands before fading into darkness. The same explosions as she felt in her heart.

She struck it again, harder. Another scrape and flash. A hot spark stung her neck. Two more landed on her shift, and glowed near her thigh. She let them burn little holes. Let them threaten to burn more. Then they too died.

Again.

Harder.

This time the flint sliced through the heel of her palm. The iron scent of blood grew in the air.

Was Captain Papa watching from above? What would he say to her getting so tangled up in a tempest of feelings?

Navigate the waters at hand.

She struck the flint correctly. Heard the clean tick. After the controlled spray of sparks died away, a tiny red glow appeared on the tinder. She blew on it, coaxing it to life, watching it grow brighter with each breath, making it dance with awakening fire.

She traded the flint for the candle and brought the wick down to the glowing ember, until it caught. The room grew from dark to merely dim. The astral lamp's reservoir had been empty for months, so she placed the candle in its chamberstick and got to work at the only thing she could do to burn off energy in the middle of the night.

Scouring. Top to bottom. Scouring out the dust, dirt, and pain. Scouring everything.

She grabbed the long-handled turkey wing and thrust it like a sword into the corner cobwebs—again and again and again—tearing down every thread hidden in the crevices. Then the grime on the windowpanes she scrubbed with vinegar and newspaper. Next, she took out her fury on the furniture with the feather duster: claw arms of the sofa, parlor chairs, candle holders, frames of the silhouettes on the wall, family Bible, and lamp chimneys.

There'd be no dust allowed here. No dirt. No pain.

His finger, carving a line around her lips.

Bristle brush to the sofa cushions. Gripping the wooden handle harder than necessary. Short, firm strokes in the direction of the nap, dust rising in small puffs, catching the candlelight. Steady pressure to attack the tight weave, the tufted buttons, and the crevices where the fabric was pulled deep into the upholstery. Forearms burning. Each scratch released the musty animal scent of horsehair.

She was sweating by the time she took a damp, oiled cloth to the mantlepiece, center table, and the whatnot shelves, but the pricking threatened to return to the back of her eyelids.

Polish next.

She mixed rottenstone with oil, rubbed down the brass reservoir of the astral lamp, the matched set of candlesticks on the mantle, and the finials on the andirons until the flame gleamed again off each surface.

The deep night sky had faded to a tender blue.

She rolled and moved the two small rugs, chairs, table. Everything but the sofa. Then the real work could begin.

Sprinkling yesterday's damp tea leaves on the floor to keep the dust down, she swept from the far corners toward that blasted door he'd stood behind. Swept and swept, as rhythmically as she once used to pace the quarterdeck.

This she could do.

This kept the thoughts away.

One bucket of white sand, two of water, scrub brush, and a cloth. Taking a section at a time, her shoulders screamed as it took her full strength to work the damp sand into the floorboards, scratching the wood surface to lift out the dirt.

Gripping the wooden handle of the brush, her hands scoured away the past—the smooth swing of the sextant, the precise turn of the chronometer key, the chart lines drawing a clear distinction between safety and danger.

Ellen wiped that section of floor. Rinsed and dried it before the wood could warp. Then she worked on the next section. And the next.

Working backward. Erasing herself. The press of fatigue. Aching knees. Another section.

Another.

When she finished and dropped the cloth in the bucket, the exhaustion crashed over her like a rogue wave. She lay back against the wall, feeling the intrusion of morning, the day bringing a return of reality, and closed her eyes in fatigue.

This last move was a grave mistake.

In the dark was where the memories attacked.

THAT DAY off the coast of Delaware, navigating the *Californian* through the Hen and Chickens, fog-blind, and the responsibility all on her shoulders. Accounting for drift and set of complex currents, checking and double-checking her calculations, how terrified she'd been that she'd kill them all.

And then the fog had finally lifted, showing Lewes Harbor exactly where she'd said it would be.

She'd never felt more alive, more herself, than in that moment.

"That's my navigator," Papa had said in his ragged voice. "Sharp as a compass and twice as reliable."

The recollection hit her like a physical blow.

Papa's love, lost.

Her entire purpose—her life's calling—cut off at the knees.

And then Perk. That heartless trifler! Showing up out of nowhere, drunk and ridiculous to toy with her affections—that is, her ambitions. Seeming to offer a path back to herself—to her adventurous heart, strategic mind, and her rightful place among the stars.

But he'd turned it to ashes instantly with his impossible condition.

A vow of obedience.

Exactly what she'd sworn to herself never to do.

And why must it be required? On Captain Papa's ship, she'd been both daughter and navigator without such a vow, and had been beloved by the crew—especially after Henlopen. They'd called her Miss Ellen at table and aye, sir when she set the courses. There'd been no contradiction, then. No pretending. No paradox.

For all Perk claimed to detest primness, he was more traditional than he was willing to admit. He didn't seek a powerful partner at his side. He wanted a tame little church mouse to do his sums in private and make him look good in public.

How was that any different to how the rest of the world thought Mr. Creesy did his own books, leaving poor Mrs. Creesy to not only run the ropewalk but obey whatever ridiculous notion came into her husband's head?

Out the window, a thin band of orange had split the horizon line.

Perk hadn't offered Ellen a dream come true, but a nightmare in disguise.

Her fury returned, and she moved on to the kitchen. Pulled everything out of the pantry, piled it on the table, and took to scrubbing down the shelves.

He thought himself such a radical, yet Perk wanted Bartlett's version of a virtuous woman as much as every other man did. Someone who addressed her husband's needs. Her children's needs. Other people's needs. Not her own. Never her own. In Bartlett's world, in Perk's for that matter, for a woman to even have needs was selfish in the extreme.

But Ellen did have needs! To feel the pull of the tides again. To turn the precise mirrors and dials of a sextant. But more than that, to feel the satisfaction of hard work well accomplished, the power of her unique and successful contribution to a shared enterprise, and a sense of belonging to the only society that truly mattered—the ship's crew.

Suddenly she collapsed into a chair.

.   .   .

IT WASN'T JUST Perk who cruelly denied her needs, she realized. It was Ellen herself. Bartlett had weaseled his way inside her head, making her feel selfish for wanting more, afraid that she'd be tested by society—and most likely correct in that fear. But what had she said to herself in church about Perk? That the worst of the results was that people he didn't like, didn't like him back?

Where was her courage? Her spirit? She'd been ready to trade her power for pleasantries, her sea for security, her vibrant life for a sleepwalking death.

Ellen realized that an unseen tide had shifted under her feet. Even if a suitor could have been found deep in the territories still willing to take her, she could no more become a cabbage farmer's wife than she could stop her own heart from beating.

Perk had spoken of a natural order, but surely if such a thing existed, it was to follow one's true nature.

"Ooh!"

Mathilda startled her. "Are you making cookies? I want a big one, Ellie!"

"No, I—"

She opened the stove's firebox and stoked the embers to start the water boiling for morning tea.

"Fetch me some water from the pump, would you, Miss M?" She needed a minute to think. For the slap of her realization to process.

She couldn't go with Perk, but she couldn't stay in Marblehead either.

Her hands shook as she grabbed the wooden bowl from the shelf. A few cups of flour. The last of the molasses. Scraping the sides of the crock left her with a good-sized scoop of lard, and she found pearlash in the bottle. She could probably even unearth a nutmeg or a few cloves from the spice tin.

Nothing else in the world was clear, except this: she could make Joe Frogger cookies for Mathilda. Why in the heavens, not? Her sister had seemed well enough recovered from yesterday's danger that by bedtime she'd begged Mama for a sailing tutor, but while Ellen had no idea what she'd do with herself next, she had a strong sense that her time with Mathilda was strictly limited.

BY THE TIME her sister returned with the pail, the sky had turned from ice-blue to peach, the kitchen was beginning to warm, and she'd made good progress with the wooden spoon.

When the dough was ready, Ellen let Mathilda roll it out on the table, then showed her how to cut it into large circles with a plate, just as Mama had once shown her. Ellen also taught her sister her own twist on the process—how to eat the leftover edges when no one was looking.

Mathilda positioned herself backward on the chair, riding it like a horse, and rested one tired cheek on the rounded back. Ellen sat on the one facing her and gave her the wooden spoon to lick.

"Last night," she fixed Ellen with a miniature grown-up frown. Then, with a wisdom that belied her years, she changed the subject.

"How do the monkeys get to Salem?" she asked.

By her age Ellen had at least gone on trips with Captain Papa. Had seen some of the world beyond the Neck. The smallness of her sister's world suddenly stung her.

"The ships come across oceans," she said. "They travel to magical places where everything is different from here. And the sailors bring back little pieces of that wonder in chests and crates. Sometimes even on a shoulder."

Ellen poked her and drew a smile.

"I'd like to have a monkey," Mathilda said. "I'd name him Captain." She didn't need to explain who she meant as his namesake.

"I'm sure Papa would be right proud," Ellen said, laughter threatening to erupt from within as she imagined his actual response.

Bless me, am I to be so highly honored by a creature who flings his own poo?

"Maybe one day you can sail to Brazil and pick out your own monkey," Ellen said.

"Maybe," Mathilda said, "But first I must learn to sail."

"Yes," Ellen smiled. "You must."

Her mind filled with an impossible vision of her sister taking to the seas, climbing the rigging with the wind in her hair, viewing far off lands. The freedom to roam the world, to follow her own choices.

"Now what?" Mathilda asked, and for a moment Ellen thought she was asking about sailing, but she was looking at the cookies.

Ellen took the poker and evened out the coals in the firebox, then let Mathilda put the baking sheet in the oven.

"Now we keep a close eye on them," she said.

A PRESENCE at her back startled her and she spun around.

Had he returned?

But it was mother. Creeping about on cat feet, one hand holding her shawl, the other a hairbrush, sniffing the air as she looked from the oven to the bowl to the pulled apart pantry.

Ellen drew a long breath and planted her feet, considering how to counter whatever argument she was about to endure. She should retreat. Offer an excuse. But no movement came. No words. Her body had had enough of pretense. Whatever came now, she'd be helpless to fight.

Mama pressed a gentle hand on Ellen's shoulder, and bid her to sit. Silently, she gathered her daughter's long, wild hair in one hand.

Then she brushed.

Ellen startled, first from surprise, then from memory. How many evenings had she felt this same gentle pressure at her scalp, this soft pulling that gathered up all her snarls and tangles and smoothed them away?

Ellen felt the bristles catch and tug at each stubborn knot, as Mama worked through her unruly hair, section by section, with patient, methodical strokes. The steady rhythm sent tingles down her spine. As each tangle surrendered, her shoulders began to unlock.

She pushed the back of her head against the softness of Mama's belly, the tension in her face melting.

Mama's hand cupped the back of her head as she used to when Ellen was small—

Suddenly, tears ambushed her from behind, flooding her eyes. She tried to control the ugly twisting that seized her face, but the sobs had found their breach. A wail escaped.

She slumped in the chair. Then collapsed to the floor, palms pressing against the icy stone.

For a moment, she'd fooled herself into believing Perk could forgive her. But his revenge was his cruelest of all—dangling freedom before her, only to snatch it away.

Her head pounded, heart clanged against her ribs. Eyes clenched shut as heaving sobs escaped into the darkness.

Mathilda's little hand rested on her calf while she gasped, unable to draw enough breath to replace what was wrenched out.

Ellen, you fool! You selfish, horrible, monstrous—

She tried to swallow the pain but the loss was stubborn and deep.

The fibers of grief twisted together like three-strand rope—strengthening with each rotation.

She couldn't lose someone she loved again.

Perk. Papa. Perk again.

Herself.

The sobs cut deeper still, choking her, laying bare the utter ridiculousness of her dream of a life at sea.

What nonsensical woolgathering! Men are the navigators, Ellen! And you're not a man! But you're no woman, either. Some unholy deformation. The devil's joke.

Perk knew it as well as anyone. She was the greater fool for being drawn in by his unruly curls and his cutting blue eyes. The truth was no one wanted her.

Why would they?

The misery tunneled deep enough that it wrenched soul from body, ripping her in half. She cried like death was upon her.

Wished it was.

Mama kept her hand on Ellen's head the whole time.

Letting it come.

When the sobs finally became breaths again and Ellen managed to crack open one swollen eye, everything was exactly the same—and yet entirely different. She placed one hand on Mama's, and the other on Mathilda's.

Utterly spent, she tried to gather the energy to sit up, took a deep breath.

What was that strange smell? Like scorched sugar.

"Oh no, no, no!" she shouted, scrambling out from underneath both of them.

When she opened the oven door, acrid smoke billowed out, hugging the ceiling and turning the air bitter and sharp. The hot baking sheet clattered onto the stovetop, the carefully shaped cookies transformed into charred circles of black powder.

"I'm so sorry, Miss M." Her voice came out raspy, hand shaking at the baking disaster.

Wide-eyed disappointment flashed on Mathilda's face, but she wrestled it down and gave Ellen a thoughtful shrug.

Mama merely stepped around to open the back door and release the smoke. Then she sat in the chair and fixed her eyes on Ellen.

"It's time to make a choice, my girl," she said. "You've had precious little opportunity to put that brain of yours to use in a long while. Might be time to do so now—"

"—I know. I must leave."

The words spoke themselves before she knew she'd made the

decision, raw truth unbound from all her hopes that she could magically become someone different. Someone who belonged.

"I've been a drain on the finances long enough. Mathilda deserves ribbons and sailing lessons. And not to be nearly killed because of her wild sister's influence or scandalized by her being accused of being a strumpet in church, only to receive drunken night-time callers as if to prove the charge."

"Hold on," Mama interrupted. "You give Mathilda too little credit for having a mind of her own. She'll be punished for her behavior, not you. She owes Mr. Thompson an apology and a good bit of scraping and sanding work on his boat for all the trouble she caused. But when that's all done, I'll take her to Salem myself. On the stage."

"And teach her to sail?" Ellen pressed her luck.

Mama sighed. "If it is something that's important to her beyond the impulse of the moment, yes. I'll find a proper way for that to happen. The community is more reasonable than you think. They're not likely to say it aloud, but they know the difference between a woman's unusual talents and a distraught father's temper tantrum. I'll warrant at least half of them had a high enough opinion of Captain Creesy they were rooting for him to avoid such a permanent entanglement with Miss Bartlett. And as for last night, thanks to the volume at which that same gentleman spoke, it was quite obvious to the whole street that his intentions toward you were honorable—even if yours toward him left a little something to be desired."

"Are you saying I should have accepted? He was off his head!"

"Aye," Mama said. "Though as he saved one of my daughters yesterday and attempted to marry the other, I've a mind to be charitable and allow that he'd reason enough yesterday to overindulge."

"You'd see me marry a drunkard, then?" Ellen's thorns were back, fighting the seduction of an easy answer—and the cage it would place around her soul.

"I would not," Mama said gently. "But such is not his way in general. I'm told he's quite respectable, in fact. His previous commander called Perkins Creesy the hardest-working crewman he'd ever seen, and the officer with the best instincts for canvas."

"How on earth would you know that?" Ellen grew dizzy—fatigue, emotion, and confusion swirling in her head like eddies.

"From your father," Mama said.

Ellen fell into the chair.

Mama merely nodded at her surprise. "He kept tabs on Perkins through the shipping people he knew. I think he felt bad for how harshly the boy was punished for the Salem incident. Was right proud to hear he'd made captain."

"Papa knew? *You knew?*"

"Neither of us believed the boy's intentions were as dishonorable as everyone imagined. We thought he'd made a mistake, but a forgivable one. But you were so distraught after, we felt it best not discussed."

Ellen felt as if she was trying to calculate numbers that kept changing value in front of her.

"But yesterday before church you said that he'd been wicked, pure and simple."

"Aye," said Mama. "I did. But you'd never have gone if I told you the full truth of the matter."

Ellen blinked. Blinked again. She still failed to sum up Mama's meaning. The eddy of confusion grew into a whirlpool.

"Don't you see? I didn't take you to church yesterday to see a wedding, but to stop one."

Gooseflesh broke out across Ellen's chest. All Mama's words about letting go, had actually been designed to rile her up instead?

She took a full minute to think through the implications, and then a minute more. Mr. Sampson had been a distraction, then? Or a backup plan, perhaps? She felt a warmth grow in her chest, but the thorns were not so easily pacified.

"It couldn't work with him, Mama," Ellen said. "Perk's—"

"—Stubborn as a mule and short-tempered as Mr. Gardener's goose," Mama said. "Yes he is. He's also the worst singer this side of the Atlantic. But in the whole of your life, outside of your family, he's the only person who's truly seen the beauty of who you truly are. You two have belonged together since you were children."

Mama's lye-weathered thumbs brushed away tears Ellen hadn't realized were falling.

"I can't promise that marrying Perkins Creesy will bring you happiness, my dear girl, but I'm quite certain that nothing else will, given the world as it is," Mama said. "You're absolutely right that Mathilda deserves every happiness in this life, but so do you."

In Mama's eyes, Ellen now saw the quiet resilience of a woman who'd weathered her own share of gales.

"You're the navigator," Mama said. "What other course could possibly steer you to a satisfied life?"

One that didn't require her to *obey* Perk as a husband, Ellen thought.

She could follow a captain's orders, of course. All sailors did. But a crew's obedience—however total it may have been at sea—was a limited agreement that covered a single voyage. It was renewed only as desired by both parties.

Marriage obedience was demanded of women alone. It was total, and it was for life. He would own her. All her thoughts and desires, her very soul—for as long as she lived.

No, the course Ellen needed to steer was one that would take her back to sea but not force her subservience to a husband.

And the only way that could ever happen—

Finally, a plan began to form. A desperate one that she calculated had almost zero chance of success, and yet was her only hope.

Ellen glanced out the back window. The dawn was becoming day. The steamer would be departing soon enough, and a choice must be made. She waited for Mama to say more. For a lecture. For direction. But none came.

Here, after all, was a taste of the independence she so desired.

Ellen wiped her palms across her eyes, pulled the shawl around her shoulders and leaned back against the chair to take it all in, to let the whirlpool settle into a shape she could recognize.

Letters wouldn't be enough. She'd have to get herself to New York in person, and the only way she could possibly do that was to face Perk again. Quite possibly the hardest thing she'd ever had to face.

"You're right, Mama," Ellen said. She stood and brushed herself off. It would be cruel to concern her mother with the dangers of her actual plan, and it certainly wasn't one she wanted Mathilda taking any ideas from. So she followed her wicked lie from ten years ago with another.

"It's a good offer. I expect I'll take it."

"You tell that man he'll have my endless gratitude for saving both my daughters," Mama said.

Mathilda threw her arms around Ellen. "Bring me back a monkey," she said.

10

The steamer moved underneath Perk all wrong. No give and take with the swells like a proper ship. The *Essex Maid* was beamy as a sow. Rather than riding waves, she shouldered them aside. Every minute or so a larger hard collision with a wall of water shuddered through her hard enough to bite into Perk's aching head.

Forward-larboard, forward-forward-forward-larboard. Eyes closed, he felt the changes in her motion, felt the ship near the harbor's exit at Fort Sewell. Anything to occupy his mind, to keep him from thinking about Marblehead and the people in it.

He actually welcomed each unsettling slide that bore him further away from the godawful rat's nest of feelings, and closer to his real life. His ordered life. To the *Oneida*'s familiar decks. To a rhythm of watches, certain as the tides.

Being at sea was a safer harbor than any port he'd ever known.

But today, even that prospect couldn't still the hammering in his heart. For all he'd put heart and soul into his career—determined to be the first man to turn to for watches and the only one who never complained, never made trouble, never hesitated—he'd not have the opportunity much longer. Not without a better record,

Somehow he'd done just brilliantly enough as first mate to fool both Howland and himself that he was ready for his own command. Perk hadn't realized just how much he'd relied on the old man until he was left on his own with a logbook and a sextant. No one to set the courses but himself.

A knock surprised him.

He hoped it wasn't a soul-saver looking to unburden him. More likely, the steward to tell him the dining hours.

He'd barely cracked the door when the wind hit him, tossing a fistful of cold drizzle in his face. The engine's chuff and paddle's churn hammered in his ears at full volume. He tasted coal in the air. Scowling, he threw the door wide, intent on—

Ellen.

Her cheeks were scrubbed raw by the wind, the collar of her coat fringed with ice. His throat closed around words he couldn't let himself say. Ellen, looking more adrift than he'd ever seen her. Lugging a basket full of . . . were those clothes?

Perk's hands fought to remain at his sides, unsure whether to haul her close or slam the door hard enough to rattle her teeth.

She took a ragged breath. "I don't mean—"

The wind tore the rest from her mouth. Her bonnet sat askew on her head, ties flapping in the wind. Her hazel eyes were dull as a mudflat.

The steamer made the turn toward Children's Island and the chill wind cut through Perk's coat. She'd be feeling it raw out there, he realized.

Still, what rose in his throat, what he wanted to say was far from charitable.

Absolutely not, Ellen Prentiss.

By God, it would serve her right. But his gut twisted. Damned if he didn't already regret what he was about to do.

He stepped back to give her space to enter.

She hesitated at the threshold, suddenly smaller than he remembered, more timid. The sight of her momentary indecision sparked something less frigid within him.

"Well, come in then," he said.

Fool! He heard Father scream in his ears.

When he closed the door and shut out the howling wind, the cabin seemed to shrink, trapping them in a pocket of heated air thick with the smell of wet wool.

For the second time that morning, Perk jammed himself into the confounded chair that barely spanned his thighs so a lady could take the bunk.

'Weak' was the gentlest curse Father would have thrown at him. He'd have found far fouler ones if he knew Perk's pulse was surging every which way. Then, when he realized he'd already been humiliated as thoroughly as possible, the anxiety was suddenly replaced with exhaustion.

"What in God's name, El?"

Then he noticed an odor. Something he was trained to respect above all else on any ship.

"Do I smell smoke?"

He shot to his feet. The nearest longboat was just outside the dining saloon. He'd have to move fast, pull a good distance before the fire reached the boiler and it blew. He recalled stories of the *Moselle* in Cincinnati. The *Pulaski* off the Carolina coast. Fewer than half survived.

But Ellen was waving him down. "You probably do," she said. "But it's not the steamer. It's me."

She yanked her bonnet off, raking her fingers through her long, brown locks, getting caught in tangles just before her ears. Perk's hand moved before a thought could bridle it, all the times he'd freed the snarls in her hair. His fingers grazed hers against her scalp, and the world hung still for a breath.

Then the impropriety of it hit him, along with the memory of her words. He snatched his hand back as if burned, nearly upsetting her basket in his clumsiness.

A blush rose on Ellen's cheeks as she finished the task herself. "I believe there's smoke in my hair," she explained.

"Oh?" Fire he would have known how to deal with, but not Ellen in his cabin. He planted himself back in the chair. "May I ask what it's doing there?"

Her mouth twisted. After all that had broken between them, what new thing could she be trying to hide now?

"I burned the Joe Froggers."

The notion of Ellen baking cookies was about as likely as Pastor Bartlett leading a band of pirates. A bark of laughter escaped before Perk could bite it back.

Then the memory of that damned door slamming stung him and he swallowed the sound.

"I see."

But the laugh had no shame. It rattled on inside him, skittering like a toad in a well until it hopped free again.

Ellen bent her head, but not before he glimpsed the smile she was trying desperately to hide.

"Stop!"

"What? You took a turn in the kitchen. How could that be unusual? Is the house still standing?"

Another sigh, but this one was followed by a smile.

"Barely."

Their eyes locked. Too much solid history, too much foggy uncertainty. His gut twisted with old wounds, chest grew tight with something like hope. Had she changed her mind? *Had he?*

"Why have you come, Ellen?"

Her gaze fell, and she worried the bonnet's ribbon in her lap while he braced himself, unsure if a blow or an embrace was about to land.

"I can't marry you, Perk, if that's what you're asking."

Lie! You could have. You chose not to. The truth of it sat like a stone in his belly, heavy and cold.

"I can't marry anyone."

What did that even mean? Was that meant to be a balm for the festering wound she'd left him with?

"I need to get to New York. And I wondered. Maybe. If you wouldn't mind . . ."

Damn her audacity. And damn his weakness for even considering it. He should never have opened the door. He dug his fists into his eyes to twist out Father's voice.

"Are you asking me—of all people—to escort you to New York?"

"In a way. I suppose. That is—"

"—The man you just dismissed with such contempt—" How dare she? The relentless vibration of the steamer rattled him from his boots to his teeth, and he couldn't finish the sentence without saying something vile out loud.

I apologize for that. Really, it—"

"—Not exactly asking, either. Are you? Showing up like a stowaway? Not giving me much choice."

"—impossible what you asked of me—"

Her words landed poorly. He didn't hear more for the discordant ringing in his ears. Impossible for her to consider marrying him. "Stop! Just stop!"

Was it his cursed weakness? Because he'd beat it out of himself if he had to. Damn her eyes!

The infernal chuffing, and the smoke, and the conversation—he was sideslipping more than the *Essex Maid*. The black space behind his eyelids swam with spiraling red dots that held no more refuge than the cabin itself.

What could he do? The steamer would stop for two hours in

Boston on the way to New York. He could set her ashore there. Let her take the stage home. It's not like she wouldn't deserve it.

Absolutely not, Ellen Prentiss.

IT TOOK several minutes for the tremor in his hands to still, for the world to stop its damned rocking. When his lids finally lifted, he saw a sight that knocked the wind clean out of him.

Ellen looked a breath away from weeping.

And in that single moment, the carefully stacked grievances, the words he'd been honing like a blade, the fight that had been coiled tight as a mainspring—all slackened and gave way.

He could see that there were actually no choices left. That he'd end up sleeping on this infernal chair tonight so she could have the bunk. That this was not the end of the favors he would grant her. That fool that he was, he would be her friend for another twenty-four hours.

Then he would sail away from her forever.

She shifted on the bunk, and their knees bumped in the tight space. For a heartbeat, neither of them moved away. The contact felt as natural as breathing, as familiar as the deck beneath his feet.

Then Ellen cleared her throat and tucked her skirts closer, while Perk pressed his back against the chair until the wood spindles bit into his spine.

The easy friendship of memory warred with this new, dangerous awareness between them. The air charged before a storm.

"What happened?" he asked. It wasn't a question as much as a surrender.

The wainscoting behind her quivered with the ship's endless thrum as she stroked the ribbon. Not toying now, but clinging. Instead of answering his question, she asked one of her own.

"Do you ever feel trapped, Perk?"

All the time. Right now, for instance.

He didn't answer, but he didn't think he was supposed to.

"As if you've fallen through the ice and been swept along and can't find your way back out again? Like you're drowning and can see the glow of the sky just above you, but you can't reach it? Can't take a breath?"

She wound the ribbon like a satin noose around her wrist.

Ellen and Perk had shared dreams and plans, games and quests, laughs and even fears, he realized, but they'd never once spoken like this.

His throat grew tight. He felt pressure—no, more than that—he felt a mandate to respond, but didn't have the slightest clue what to say.

"All this time," she continued, "What I thought I wanted most in the world was to be at sea. Then when you showed up and offered it to me, I realized there was something I needed even more."

She grew quiet and he waited for her to tell him what that was. But she winced and threw the bonnet hard in the corner, startling him with her strength. Or was it fury?

"I know I don't deserve the time of day from you. That there's no apology big enough to make up for the lie I told after our trip to Salem, Perk. I've been haunted by what I did for ten full years, after all you—"

A bolt of fury surprised Perk. But then something else struck him harder: Ellen Prentiss, admitting a wrong. The confession cost her— he could see it in the way her shoulders hunched, how she couldn't quite meet his eyes. He wasn't sure what to do with this new, more human version of her.

Her hand went to her throat and she sat in silence for a full minute before she spoke again. "I was such a coward, so afraid of losing my position. . . . But I don't mean to make excuses for my wickedness." She swallowed hard. "It was the biggest mistake of my life."

Her voice was so soft, so unlike the Ellen he knew, that he almost didn't hear her. In that moment, something in him yielded, the years of resentment beginning to crack like spring ice.

"Asking for your forgiveness might be the second biggest," she said with the hint of a grin before she shrunk further into herself. "After all I cost you. I know you're not much for the idea of divine providence, but maybe it'll change your mind to learn I ended up stuck on land where everyone else thinks I belong."

"Only one thing you can be sure of, El," Perk said.

She looked up suddenly, her eyes so full of pleading, he wavered on whether to finish. But the silence was too awkward to endure.

"Wasn't your prowess in the kitchen that kept you on land."

A tear escaped, tracing a path down her cheek. But also a smile. Wan at first, it grew tentative as a hermit crab emerging from its shell. Just a little, but it was enough that he didn't want to ask: If it wasn't the sea she wanted on the other side of that ice, then what was it? What was keeping her from breathing?

"I believe I'm bound to express my gratitude to you for pointing out such an obvious certainty. Is that right, Captain Creesy?"

'My pleasure,' he wanted to say, but thought she might take it wrong. "Don't mention it."

"No," she said, half-hiding a sniffle. "I think I won't."

After a moment, she chuckled. "How about I make you a fair trade?" She wiped her cheek. "You asked me for navigation lessons. If you'll escort me to New York, I'll take every minute between here and the North River to teach you what I know."

"For all the good that'll do."

"Well, maybe none," she said, a spark flickering in her eye. "But I highly doubt that, Perkins. Don't forget that I know you. You're smarter than you think. You always have been."

The warmth that slammed into his chest caught him off guard. He swallowed hard, the unfamiliar praise sticking in his throat like half-chewed salt pork. He hadn't the slightest idea how to respond, so he did what he always did: ignored it.

"Then what?"

"Well, then you can go off and win one of your races. What else?"

"No. I mean, then what for you?"

Her slow blink sent a prickle up the back of his neck. She was building a wall, brick by brick, behind her gaze. Years of charting her moods told him that much. He glanced at her basket for a hint of the truth. A pile of clothes, a leather book, and a spyglass. Her reticule was flat enough to be empty, or nearly so.

"I have a plan," she said, swallowing. Each word seemed to cost her something.

She'd always been the planner, but there was nothing Perk could see that suggested her plan was viable this time.

"I'll get a pair of trousers and a cap. Cut my hair and join a crew as a ship's boy. I figure as Elliot Prentiss, I could—" The words caught in her throat. "—could find my own way aboard a ship."

SHE WANTED TO SAIL, then. Any tub. Any ratcatcher of a crew. Any one but his. Because she knew him too well.

He studied her face, the desperate lines etched into her forehead. Her hazel eyes, the soft curve of her cheek. How to tell her this wouldn't hold? That even the *Essex Maid*'s deckhand, scrawny as a gull, had more of a man's look about him? That maybe there were some who could pull it off, but not her. She was too—what was the damn word? Not beautiful, exactly. Beauty was a polished look that Ellen had never chased. But there had always been a pull to her, even as a girl. A directness that had snagged his attention. A bloom too bright for—

She was no Elliot.

And what if she managed, impossibly, to get hired on? Ellen had never taken a belaying pin to the head, never squared off against a knife, hadn't the strength to haul in the bucking canvas of a topsail in a gale. And Lord help her if they discovered she was a woman—the mere thought of what they might do to her. . . . His hands made fists before he knew it, knuckles grinding.

What to do?

She'd thrown his proposal back in his face and he knew she'd sooner starve than take a penny from him. A gift, though . . . would she refuse a gift? Could he trick her into taking something worth a few months' board, something she could sell easy enough for cash?

A watch, maybe? If only he carried something so fancy.

"Tell me what you'd like to know," Ellen said.

His mind raced with all manner of questions. *Why you lied? If you ever cared for me at all? Who will look out for you?*

"—About navigation," she added, seeming to read his mind as always.

He settled against the chair back. The image of her swallowed by that city, adrift without him, tightened his chest.

"I'm not sure where to start," he admitted.

The air moved easier in his lungs after those words. He hadn't noticed the knot in his chest until it loosened, but he could feel it now.

Still, half of him remained braced, ready for a blow, and he knew it wouldn't shift until he'd seen Ellen off, as safe as he could manage, in New York.

"Captain Nat holds the record time to market," Perk said. "106 days from Canton. Dumaresque is next at 109, Waterman at 114." He took a deep breath and continued. "In five years under Howland's command, we were never slower than a respectable 130 days, save when we lost the foremast and limped into Anjer under a jury rig. Not good enough for glory, exactly, but respectable enough for Grinnell."

His throat tightened thinking of the humiliating results printed in black ink in the *Mercantile Gazette* for every shipper to see.

ARRIVALS: Bark ONEIDA, Capt. Creesy, 173 days from Canton with teas, silks, and china ware to Grinnell, Minturn & Co

ARRIVALS: Bark ONEIDA, Capt. Creesy, 169 days from Canton

ARRIVALS: Bark ONEIDA, Capt. Creesy, 182 days from Canton

He tried to tell himself that in twenty-four hours, he'd never see Ellen again. But of all people to humiliate himself in front of—yet she was also the only person on earth who might help him improve his speed.

"My best so far is 169," he finally said.

He thought the confession would feel like death, but it actually eased the tension in his shoulders to jaw it out, just as it had with Henry.

And it reminded him that in all the time he'd been a mate, he'd always imagined the triumph of having his own command, the satisfaction of having people clip to his orders, but had never once considered how impossible it would be to share worries or doubts—or failures—with another living soul.

"Grinnell's been kind enough to remind me, on several occasions, that his tea business is not a charity. Finally he gave me an ultimatum. If I don't make it to Canton in less than 130 days this time, I'll no longer have a ship to command. He'll give the *Oneida* to my weasel of a first mate. For all the good it'll do either of them."

There. Done. The whole sorry story.

"So you need to shave 39 days off your best time," Ellen said, getting to the heart of it as always. He waited for her to tell him it was impossible.

But she continued. "Tell me more. What were your daily runs with Howland like?"

He struggled to pull a figure out of memory.

But Ellen didn't need to wait for his answer, working it through for herself. "If you regularly made New York in 130 days," she said, "And the route from Canton is around 15,000 nautical miles give or take, you would have done 110- and 115-mile days on average. Does that sound about right?"

Perk nodded, hating how easily she commanded the knowledge he'd struggled for years to master. Hating even more how much he needed that knowledge.

"And what are your dailies on the *Oneida*?"

Finally, a point of pride. "When we get decent wind, I can move her faster than Howland's *Horatio*, and she's an older, smaller ship."

Ellen nodded as if he was merely validating what she already knew. She didn't seem to notice the achievement it took to get a shorter, stubbier vessel to move through the water as fast as—

"You're going as fast or faster but arriving 39 days later. So you're either sailing an extra 3,000 miles or missing the trade winds entirely. Probably a combination of both."

"I knew it wasn't good, but—"

"—I take it your mate isn't a very skilled navigator either?"

Perk shook his head. "Grinnell's cousin. Not much of a sailor either, truth be told, but I've little choice in the matter."

"So we need to find you an effective course that'll put you in the favorable winds and currents or you won't have a prayer."

His blood was up now. "As I said, I could do with some navigational tips—"

"You don't need tips, Perk. You need a navigator."

He clenched his fist under the table, but she continued before he could react.

"Sorry," she said. "I just—I want you to win. I want to help you solve this and I don't know where to start since the problem is so—"

"Impossible. Ridiculous," he admitted. "All of it. Me playing at being captain, especially."

"Oh, Perk! Not ridiculous at all," she said. "You're a tremendous captain. I know you are, probably better than anyone. Apparently Papa was quite proud of what you'd achieved, and you know that man didn't suffer fools. It's just your route that's confusing me. I'm trying to work out if it's more of a position error or a strategy problem. To get you to Canton in 130 days, I think it will be helpful to break the voyage down into three separate legs and look at each one separately.

"First, New York to the Cape of Good Hope. Second, Good Hope to the Sunda Strait. And finally, Sunda to Canton."

SHE CONTINUED TALKING, though he lost the thread of it, focused on the stunning announcement that her father had been proud of him when his own could not. After the swell in his chest finally eased, he saw her sitting there as he hadn't before.

The exact same Ellen, only older. And him, the exact same boy he thought he'd left behind.

She hadn't come because she cared for him. Didn't want to be his wife. She'd come because she had no choice, and that thought burned worse than her rejection.

But watching her there, proud chin lifted even as her hands twisted nervously in her lap, he realized something that surprised him: he'd help her anyway. Because somewhere deep in their past were two children who'd once promised to sail the world together.

Father didn't deserve his help, and Mother and Patience didn't need it.

But Ellen did.

At least for this. The thought was as welcome as it was pathetic. It felt good to be useful to someone. He could turn her down, of course. Chase her off the steamer when it stopped in Boston.

But he knew he wouldn't. He'd made his choice.

He needed her as well.

"There's a map on the wall in the dining saloon," he heard himself say. "Shall we begin?"

11

When Boston Harbor hove into view through the dining salon window, Ellen set down her pencil, pulled on her bonnet, and braved the spitting sleet to stand at the rail.

"It's only a short stop," Perk said, buttoning his coat behind her. "We'll have to be quick about it."

Gripping the rail through shallow breaths of coal dust, she barely heard him, struck by an unexpected flutter in her chest—a sensation she'd thought long dead. But as it buzzed to life like awakening bees, she realized it had merely been dormant.

Joy.

The *Essex Maid* joined the skiffs and dories crisscrossing the water, steaming toward the forest of masts that ringed the city front like a necklace. Black-hulled schooners. Green-hulled barkantines. Ships with bare yards, awaiting cargo. Others with sails bent on, ready to depart.

The *Californian* hadn't made a run to Boston in years, and Ellen noticed a much wider array of flags than she remembered: the Empire of Brazil, the Republic of Texas, Hawaiian Kingdom.

Some she didn't even recognize. Uruguay? The Kingdom of Sardinia?

Perk reached for the same spot on the rail and two of his fingers accidentally overlapped hers for a moment before he pulled them away, leaving her with a hint of warmth she couldn't help but treasure.

But she mustn't let herself get caught up in such feelings.

SHE HAD her own mission in Boston—to reconnect with herself. To remember what it was to be Ellen Prentiss, the navigator.

Years ago, she could have named every quay. Much of that knowledge had faded like calico left in the sun, but she could still remember the biggest ones.

Long Wharf held court as the center of the Boston docks, stretching almost a half mile from the harbor to State Street. Central Wharf sat to its south and T-Wharf to the north—so tight that when the winds were contrary, Captain Papa'd been forced to warp the *Californian* around docked ships to reach their berth.

Unlike Marblehead, with its many complicated memories, her recollections of Boston were simple and wondrous. The first big city she'd ever seen, where a dozen languages could be heard at one time and women carried parasols midweek, and Broad Street spread wide enough to race four carriages abreast.

The city called to her like a siren. Two hours wouldn't be nearly enough to revisit all her lovely ghosts. That spring walk through the Commons, sunlight filtering through the swaying trees, making the grass seem to move like the sea. Or the bookstore on Cornhill Street, with its worn floorboards, musty-sweet scents of leather bindings and fresh ink, and the proprietor scratch-scratching his pen nib as he made notes in his ledger.

The semaphore station rose up from the foot of Central Wharf, dressed in a new coat of paint. Ellen could spend the whole two hours of their visit right there. Papa had taken her into that three-story watchtower once because she'd been curious about the system of flags that alerted a city full of merchants, insurers, customs officials, and family members when a ship was spotted through their powerful telescope.

The old captains who manned it had been patient enough with her questions, even if perplexed by a young girl's interest. A white flag hoisted on the left pole meant a merchantmen, she remembered with a smile, and white on the right meant a packet. Red flag for a warship, blue for a whaler. Two flags meant a foreign vessel. Yellow for sickness. Half-mast if it appeared in distress.

She knew they hadn't believed Papa when he told them she'd navigated them into port, but their laughter had led to one of the most special moments of her life—

"No time to stare, Ellen," Perk tugged at the sleeve of her coat, his voice laced with an irritating blend of concern and authority. "You've filled my head with calculations. Now it's my turn to return the favor."

Perk was giving her far too much credit. She'd barely begun with the navigation lessons, and he was proving a very slow student. But she also hadn't asked him for help beyond transport to New York, and didn't want more.

"We've got but two hours to make you a boy, since no one's ever heard of a ship's girl," he added.

She tried to tunnel back to her semaphore memory, where she'd watched the official chronometer tick down the seconds toward noon.

Five minutes out, they'd let her—fourteen-year-old Ellen Prentiss —hoist the black timekeeping ball to the top of the pole. At the same time, on the deck of every departing vessel in the harbor—whether headed for Calcutta, Nuku Hiva, Muscat, Zanzibar, or Valparaíso—a captain stood with his eyes fixed on her ball, his fingers on his chronometer, waiting to synchronize with her signal.

The weight of responsibility was almost beyond her imagining. A mere two seconds off could mean two nautical miles of error—easily the difference between a ship safely making port and going down with all hands lost. Their lives were literally in her hands. She was nearly shaking with nerves, readying for the drop as they counted down the last seconds, hoping not to mess up—

"Come," Perk said. "I've an old friend we can call on."

Shush! She wanted to say. *I'm not a pup to follow you in tow.*

The semaphore men had called "Now!" in unison. She'd let go of the rope, breathless with fear she'd done it wrong. But then one of the old captains gave her a congratulatory thump on the back. She was elated with relief, but even more by the fact that in the excitement, he'd forgotten she was a girl.

"We'll get you a proper slops chest."

What was she, a dressmaker's dummy? As the *Essex Maid* docked at Long Wharf, she rubbed feeling back into her fingers, warmed by the memory, then saddened by it.

Back then, her future had felt as wide as the horizon line.

"I can look out for myself, Perk," she said. She'd never admit the ferry ticket had all but emptied her reticule.

But also, she realized there was a place, a ghost of a memory, that she wanted to visit even more than the semaphore station. Familiar, beloved, untouchable. Anything to put off thoughts of the challenges that awaited her in New York as long as—

"—This way." Perk's hand was firm on her elbow as he strode down the gangplank, shoulders squared, jaw set, ready to take charge. "If we hurry, we may have just enough time."

For all she appreciated his help, she didn't want it. But what could she tell him? That for the first time in her life, she had no real plan except to place one foot in front of the other? Her future was a compass needle, spinning wildly, looking for direction but finding none.

Memory was at least a fixed destination, and she wanted nothing more than to travel to those silent places inside her head where Captain Papa still lived and she was still his navigator—but Perk kept tugging her away. No matter how good his intentions, he was clumsily, arrogantly, trampling on her soul. The words burned in her throat: *Leave me be.*

The snow was falling, soft and thick so that even the well-trodden wharf was covered in a sheen of white. Luckily, the crispness of the air reduced the unmistakable harbor smells of tar, fish, sewage, and rum.

Ellen glanced about for a monkey, but the wharves felt more clean-shaven than she remembered. Fewer tarred pigtails, more cropped hair and jaunty scarves. Less of the old sea-dog look, and more like clerks playing dress-up. It also felt more hemmed in.

Though perhaps that wasn't Boston, but the limited perspective allowed by her hat. *Bonnet.* The last time she'd been here, she'd been young enough that Papa let her travel with her head and hair free.

"Breeches, to start."

Ellen could see she'd have no chance of peace today. Perk would be her protector whether she wanted saving or not. Given the painful fact that she was in his debt for escorting her to New York, there was precious little she could do about it.

Thank heaven she'd be rid of him tomorrow.

She took three more steps and then her legs nearly gave out.

Rid of him—until when?

She might have fallen if he'd not steadied her elbow.

After they parted in New York, when would she see Perk again? Her mind caught in a slipping loop trying to create a situation likely to lead to a reunion, but she couldn't get past the near certainty of the answer.

Never.

"And clearly you need better boots if you want to stay on the boat side of the ocean," he continued, as her mind continued to reel. "Perhaps we need to craft a convincing tale of a daring escape from Barbary pirates to seal the deal?"

His voice was light, but his eyes darted anxiously to the rough-looking sailors lounging near the docks, and his shoulders tensed. They both knew what kind of danger awaited a young woman alone on the docks, with no money and no prospects.

His attempt at humor faded, and when he spoke again, his words were raw with concern. "Ellen, it's not just the sea that's merciless. If they take you for a jack, that's a hard enough life. But if you're discovered—"

"—Is that your best attempt at a rallying speech?" She swallowed the pain, too worried his concern would grow oppressive. "Because if so, Captain, we should work on that more than your disastrous navigation."

His forehead creased for a heartbeat before he blinked away whatever thoughts crowded his mind, then his eyes brightened with forced cheer.

"Oh no," he said. "That's just me being conversational. You want thoughtful words of encouragement? Why didn't you say so? Belay that chatter and step lively, you slack-jawed lubber! Pick up the pace or you'll be dining on salt horse for a month!"

She had to laugh. His arm wrapped around hers, pulling her shoulder into his, reminding her of the feather-light touch of his finger on her lips in the dark of night. "That's not quite—"

"—Blast your eyes, if you're caught flat-footed again you'll taste the cat! Now, I want every brass fitting polished until it blinds the gulls!"

"I only meant—"

"What? This is good practice for you."

"Aye," she said to shut him up.

"Aye, Cap'n!"

"Aye, Captain," she surrendered. "Whatever you command, my —" But even joking about such submission got caught in her throat and she was glad for the bustle of State Street that saved her from completing it.

THEY WERE QUICKLY CAUGHT up in the flow of carts, carriages, and someone trying to corral a drift of piglets back into a broken cage. Everyone moved with a frantic energy, a sense of purpose that bordered on desperation. The days of leisurely bartering and story-telling seemed long gone.

Ellen searched for the chandlery she'd last visited, but it was also gone. Replaced by something called *The Mariner's Emporium*, that sported a gaudy painted sign and a window full of cheaply made goods. Around it, new granite warehouses and construction expanded in every direction she could see.

She'd been away seven years, and yet it felt like seven lifetimes had passed on without her.

"Come on," he said, raising his voice to compete with the clatter of wheels and voices bouncing off the cobbles and the brick insurance buildings.

"Where are we going?" She got no answer, but Perk tugged her out of the way of a pair of horses drawing an omnibus. Even with blinders on, the horses could likely see better than she could.

As she spun around, Ellen caught a glimpse of a woman boarding the bus in a bonnet at least two hands long, so festooned with pink flowers and green ribbons she couldn't see a hint of the face who bore it.

How did she manage? For that matter, how did she move under that heavy bell of petticoats that made even Euphemia look like a provincial bumpkin?

But Ellen hadn't long to wonder. Perk's pace was relentless and with her arm tight in his she was nearly running to keep up with his long stride. He'd murder her in a game of tag today, she thought.

The crowd was thinner near the print houses on Chatham and

Ellen's heart beat faster as they neared the familiar realm of Kilby Street. The joy of what had happened a mere block away almost brought a dance to her step. The streets met up at odd angles so she couldn't see the building, but the precious memory traveled to meet her anyway.

THE ATHENAEUM. That smell of old books, the creak of the velvet-covered chairs, and the hushed anticipation before her very first lecture: *Discoveries in Celestial Mechanics*. The content had been fascinating, but the discussion afterward carved an everlasting place in her heart.

While the old captains at the semaphore station had been kind, they'd thought her navigation little more than a doting father's lark. But at the Athenaeum, a midshipman had actually asked her for her opinion of his idea to standardize ships' logs in order to discover patterns in the data. He'd accepted her, a girl, as his mathematical equal.

She'd returned to the *Californian* with a head so full of ideas that she'd began to craft her own data tables with titles such as *Leeway, As Measured in Varying Wind and Sea States*, and *Boat Speed Logged by Wind Force and Sail Configuration*.

Pure data that yielded useful insights, improved her accuracy, and in the blinding fog of the Hen and Chickens, was the very thing that had saved them from the shoals.

All of her data had been lost with the schooner, of course. But the Athenaeum was the first place outside Papa's schooner where she'd felt like she belonged, exactly as she was.

No one there scolded her to choose a pleasanter subject for discourse, to stop fidgeting, or use arsenic creams to erase the tan from her face. No one tried endlessly to help her attract a husband. She was accepted merely for following her own inclinations.

This was the feeling she was trying to return to.

And now, here she was, a mere block away, and she'd lost the ability to set her own course. Instead, a strong arm directed—commanded—her to follow his lead.

This is what she'd never be able to explain to Perk. He'd always seen the box others were trying to stuff her into, but was equally blind to the one of his own creation. She couldn't have anyone—even Perk—dictate her choices, decide what was acceptable and what wasn't.

To gain the sea without freedom would merely be to endure the same trapped land life she'd just fled—only wetter.

But when they reached the end of the block, Perk placed a hand on the small of her back to turn her toward a building, and instead of pulling away, she allowed herself the tiny luxury of lingering in his touch a moment longer than strictly necessary.

HYPOCRITE, Ellen chastised herself, but she followed Perk's pointed finger, and couldn't hold in her gasp. Through a window framed in weathered blue clapboard stood a gleaming sextant resting on a wooden tripod.

Such a sight would have brought a spark of joy regardless, but this wasn't just any sextant.

She stepped closer, pulse quickening, fingers already itching to lift it from its resting place on the other side of the glass. No common navigator's tool, battered from years at sea. No wooden-framed relic like the one she'd used on the schooner, with its sluggish vernier readings and mirrors that fogged with the first hint of spray.

This was a master's instrument—a solid brass frame, slender and precise, its polished arc divided to the sharpest degree with an inset silver scale, its mirrors held in place by screws finer than a tailor's needle.

And the telescope—God, the telescope. A proper three-draw achromatic lens, not some shoddy, distorted thing. The stunning instrument probably cost half a year's wages.

Perk was grinning with satisfaction. "I'd a feeling you'd like this place."

She looked at the sign above the window where 'Delano's Chandlery and Nautical Outfitters' was painted in crisp, golden letters against a background of deep blue.

It could just as easily have spelled out 'Heaven.'

"Old Man Howland taught me there are two people to make friends with on land," Perk said. "One is whatever old sod who runs your shipping house. The other is the best chandler you can find."

The bell tinkled as Perk ushered her into the warmth of the small shop. The smells were immediately so familiar, so treasured. Hemp. Tar. Salt. Brass polish.

The dusty windows barely allowed in enough light to see the organized chaos of the shop, but she'd spent enough time in chandleries to know immediately that this one was special.

A row of battered octants lined the back wall. Beneath them, a slate, still smudged with chalk, leaned against an open barrel full of nautical charts, rolled and carefully tied with twine.

Perk called out a hearty "Hallo," and Ellen followed him around the coils of cordage, careful not to hit her head on one of the many blocks hanging from the ceiling.

"Ah, Creesy, is it?"

The voice behind a heap of sailcloth was gravelly and warm, and she followed the sound to find a man in a practical brown waistcoat and rolled sleeves. His thick white mustache was slightly yellowed at the edges. Behind him several cutlasses hung by their hilts from iron pegs, blades catching the soft light.

"Been a damned while. Heard you've got your own command now."

"A 750 tonner," Perk answered, unable to hide the glow of pride that reddened his cheeks.

"Well earned, I'm told. Captain Howland still won't shut up about you saving the ship in a storm off Anjer. Says he knew right then you'd make captain afore you made thirty."

Ellen thought back to their discussion on the steamer. What had Perk said about limping into Anjer under jury rig? He'd certainly never mentioned heroics.

"Howland was a great teacher, and I was damn lucky to be his mate. Meantime, may I introduce you to my friend, Miss Eleanor Prentiss."

Ellen felt a sudden rush of warmth at his choice of words. Could they indicate a hint of forgiveness?

Perk might have made a good husband, she thought suddenly, for they'd been the closest of friends for a decade. But she kicked herself for the thought. Probably it would have been a disaster. She'd been his enemy just as long.

"And Miss Prentiss," Perk continued, "May I present the legendary Captain Delano, retired, of the *Patrick Henry*. When I showed up here as naught but a ship's boy, knowing nothing about nothing, he's the one that taught me to box a compass. It's thanks to him I made my way forward of the mast."

There was a confidence in Perk's description of the past that Ellen didn't recognize from the time. Almost a joy. She imagined him coming in here as the Perk she'd once known—the beat-down boy who could never please his father—and memorizing the 32 compass points forward and back: north, north by east, north-northeast, northeast by north . . .

She'd flattered herself back then that she was the only one to bring out that light in his eyes, but now she saw fully what hubris that was. Perk was his own man. He always had been.

"Pleasure, Miss," Delano said. "And little enough help he needed from me. Never seen such a young man could splice a line like an old salt."

Perk shook his head, deflecting praise. "Don't let this cozy shop full of odds and ends fool you, El. He's as tough a jack as they come. Still holds the record for the fastest westbound Atlantic crossing at a mere 15 days."

"No point boring a lady about some dusty old voyage, long forgot."

"Could be such," Perk said, eyeing Ellen. "But it's hard to say. You might be surprised about this particular lady. Maybe you recall her father, Captain Prentiss of the *Californian*."

"Course I do," Delano's eyes lit up. "Right sorry to hear of his loss, too. Brightened up half of Boston with that laugh of his." He paused and turned to Ellen. "Well, then. That wouldn't make you the lass that navigated his ship through Cape Henlopen in the fog, would it?"

Ellen's cheeks reddened as she gave him a modest nod.

"Then it's very much my pleasure to make your acquaintance. What was it he used to say about you? Sharp as a compass and something or other."

Twice as reliable. Ellen's heart beat so strongly, she managed only a grateful nod in return.

"Now Creesy, where'd you hide your ship? I haven't seen a 750 tonner in weeks."

"Didn't sail in this time," Perk said. "Caught the steamer. Just dropped in today to get a slops chest. That something you can help with?"

"Of course. You shipping a greenhorn?"

"Something like that. This particular sailor has some experience, but lost all their gear in a wreck and needs to start fresh. I'd say two sets of canvas duck trousers, three sturdy shirts, some thick wool stockings." He glanced at Ellen, looking her up and down. "They've got a serviceable peacoat but'll need oilskins, a sou'wester, and a pair of your best fish-oil treated hobnails. That and the regulars plate, cup, spoon, marlinspike, and a sea chest to put it in—a good one, if you can manage, with brass corners."

As Perk outlined all the gear, Ellen's stomach dropped. She had naught but a dollar or so in her reticule. His list would cost something nearer to five.

"Certainly some economy can be made," she said to Perk, trying to keep her voice low. "Maybe your sailor can make do with merely a set of trousers, for instance."

Perk turned to her, eyes flashing, though she couldn't tell whether from fear or anger.

"I believe, Miss Prentiss, you know well what would happen to our friend Elliot if he takes to sea without all the necessities. A single pair of trousers would soon enough be worn to ribbons. Without oilskins for the torrential rains, he'd be wet to the bone in minutes and freeze soon after. Without a plate, he'd not eat. No cup, he wouldn't drink. No chest, he'd not sit. And no marlinspike, he'd never be allowed aboard in the first place."

He was right, of course. Ellen's plan was no plan at all. It was a disaster in the making. The humiliation of having to admit she was broke, the possibility that Perk might feel responsible to do something more weighed increasingly on her.

He perused a stack of hats, checking the stitching and tarring until he found one he was satisfied with. "Take off your bonnet," he commanded.

Ellen glanced at Delano, but Perk explained away the connection neatly enough. "Our friend Elliot's not large. He'd be swimming in anything that fit me, but he's right about her size."

Ellen untied the bonnet laces and pulled it off her head. Immediately she had peripheral vision again, and was so grateful to have it gone, she resolved in that moment that the bonnet would never go back on her head—scandal be damned.

The sou'wester was an entirely different story. A beautiful piece of kit, coated with linseed oil and lampblack, with a short brim to catch rain in the front and shed it in the back. When she put the hat on, she found it snug and warm, but with full visibility.

No wonder Captain Papa had so rarely taken his off.

"Load of sea chests just in," Delano said, carrying one through the side door, and setting it on the counter as he carefully collected a pile of the smaller items.

"Perk—"

He leaned close to whisper. "Well you can't very well board a ship with your togs in a basket, now can you?"

"It's not that. The thing is—"

"—I've a knife. I could cut your hair on the steamer if you like," he whispered. "Got pretty good shoring fellow crewmen. Better at that than calculating, you'll be glad to hear."

"Perk!" She grabbed his arm, causing him to flinch slightly. Her mouth went dry. "I don't have the money for—for Elliot's things."

"Oh," Perk said, twisting his mouth into that thinking look she remembered from helping him with schoolwork. Then he glanced at Delano.

"Well, then Elliot's lucky to have the both of us today. Captain Delano here will give us the best prices and I'll put up the cash."

He gingerly peeled Ellen's fingers from his forearm so he could reach his vest pocket.

"But I can't let you—"

"—Elliot can pay me back later."

"But how's that possible if—if he's never going to see you again—"

When Perk winced, Ellen realized what she'd just said out loud.

Behind her, Delano coughed, but she couldn't take her eyes from Perk's face. He blinked twice. Three times.

"Don't give it another thought," he said finally. "It's a gift."

Then he leaned down and whispered, his breath hot in her ear.

"Doesn't every bride need a trousseau?"

She knew he was joking, of course. Should have scoffed. Instead, the heat of his breath at her ear sent a shiver down her spine and took the last protests from her mouth.

As he stepped to the back to have a private word with Delano, her treacherous heart—the very same one that refused to be imprisoned in a marriage—did a quick backflip before she could smother it.

She gave Perk her best smile. The only payment she had left to offer.

12

———

"After you've done that calculation, you mustn't forget to subtract the magnetic deviation . . ."

Perk's skull hammered like a loose block in heavy seas. For all of Ellen's earnest effort to wedge navigation strategies into his thick head, somewhere in the wee hours of the morning his exhausted mind had quietly given up trying to follow her trail of numbers.

He pressed his fingers to his temples, elbows braced on the table. The lamp on the wall of the dining saloon sputtered twice before dying with a thin curl of smoke. They'd drained the whale oil dry.

The gloom darkened only slightly and drew his attention to the daybreak—a crimson glow now visible through the porthole. An inauspicious sign he'd expected from the wind patters of the last few days.

Red sky at morning, sailors take warning.

It would make for a very tricky departure. He'd have to be at his best if he was to avoid a collision or running aground in this weather.

And yet he'd just gone three nights without sleep. Perk blinked as he counted back. The first night grappling with Father's demand and

Mother's seeming peril. The second too drunk to stand for his own proposal, too sick to lie down after. Then last night, spent tangled in a rat's nest of calculations that refused to settle in his mind.

No. Four nights. He'd forgotten his sleepless passage on the way to Marblehead, too. No wonder he couldn't follow spherical trigonometry. At the moment he could barely count to four.

Perk had gone without sleep before—it was as inevitable at sea as being wet. He'd served hundreds of storm watches with hands frozen to the lines. Nights pacing the quarterdeck, every nerve tuned to the weight of wind against sail.

But he wasn't out under open sky now, riding the rhythm of sea and ship. He was in an empty dining saloon, swallowing stale air and drowning in numbers he'd never be able to hold in his hands.

Ellen tapped her pencil against the table, some part of her still believing he could learn to see the world her way. He wondered if her mind was as ordered as her tables of probabilities.

He stretched out a leg, shaking off the stiffness, and let his eyes drift across the empty room, past the supper napkins discarded in limp heaps and the fly picking at a crust of bread. Through the opposite row of portholes, he could just make out the dark smudge of the city, jagged with rooftops and masts, and low scudding clouds.

Ellen remained hunched over her notes, frowning in concentration, but Perk had reached his limit. He'd just have to do his best when the time came and hope it was good enough to see him to Canton in 130 days.

Instead, he did what came naturally. He listened to the wind's howl and studied the whipped-up sea. The wind had completed its shift to the northeast and was already blowing a solid Force Seven. More than a tricky departure. Maybe Force Eight by the time the *Oneida* could get tugged out to Sandy Hook. By the time he reached the narrows, the seas would be a churned-up mess of cross swells and stinging spray, and likely to be so for days.

But this was a challenge he was made for. Perk found himself welcoming the blow, whistling quietly—the old superstition to invite more wind.

Far better a gale than a calm to move a ship.

The *Essex Maid* gave a loud creak, pulling Perk back to the morning, as the sway of her hull adjusted to the morning tide. Outside, the paddle wheels churned steady, but with less drive. He felt the drag, the shift. Like a horse being reined in. They were closing in on New York.

His MIND HAD GROWN fuzzy at the edges, but he needed to focus on what had to be done next for his departure. The timing would be tight. The steamer wouldn't reach Albany Basin until around half-past eight, but the *Oneida* was docked all the way across town on the East River and the steam tug had been booked for eleven sharp.

The tide wouldn't wait and neither would Grinnell. That left Perk naught but two and a half hours to get across town, confirm the crew were aboard and sober enough to set a sail, review the cargo manifests and provision lists, check the hold for safe stowage, and ensure they had the provisions to be self-sufficient for months on end.

If the hardtack was riddled with weevils, they'd have naught to eat but weevils. If the water spoiled, they'd die of thirst. If the sails blew out and he hadn't any canvas aboard, their deaths would be slow, and if the pumps failed without the spares to fix them, their deaths would be fast.

An hour, perhaps, to get across town. Little more than an hour and a half to check they were seaworthy. He could only hope Austin had done his work diligently. For once.

Next, he'd need to check the cargo manifests carefully. There'd be tens of thousands of dollars' worth of some goods or other in the hold that he bore full responsibility for. For the eastbound trip, the *Oneida* was likely full of cotton bales and ginseng baskets—about the only products China wanted from America—along with dozens of chests of Mexican silver. Those were necessary for the return trip—to buy the Chinese silks, porcelain, furniture, lacquer cabinets, camphorwood chests, spices, papers, and especially teas that New York's gilded mansions would fight each other tooth and nail to possess.

His jaw clenched. It would be the biggest race of his life, and if anything went wrong in the next couple hours, he'd fail to even start it.

If he got to sail her back, that was.

No doubt, Austin had spent Perk's absence sinking into the feel of command, taking liberties at his expense. Was likely watching the clock even now, hoping his captain would fail to arrive in time and that he'd get control of the ship even sooner.

A slow creak ran through the hull as the steamer adjusted course. The angle of light against Ellen's face shifted, and Perk saw the moment she registered the change. "Castle Garden," he whispered by way of good morning, nodding toward the Battery, trees lining the promenade just beyond.

She didn't hear him. Or if she did, wasn't ready to acknowledge the dawn.

"—This is the fun part, where you bring in the number from step fourteen and—"

"Ellen."

He set his hand gently over her moving pencil, pressing it still, then fought an urge to keep it there forever.

"We're here."

HER EYES MET HIS. That sharp flash of hazel. And for a second, he forgot himself. Forgot what the morning meant. Forgot that in minutes, they'd step off the ferry and walk two different paths.

She'd be alone in New York. And he'd be gone for fourteen to sixteen months. He shuddered to think what would become of her in that time. She'd not wanted to waste a moment of her instruction time changing clothes or letting him cut her hair, so she'd arrive in

New York as a woman, though with all the trappings of a man. That and a little extra he'd tucked in the sea chest to keep her from starving was the best he could do.

At the convergence of the East and North Rivers, he stood, rolling his shoulders against the ache. Then he slung his sea bag across his back, hoisted Ellen's sea chest onto his shoulder, and balanced her basket on his arm.

When he stepped toward the walkway, the harbor air struck his face as he reached the deck. New York was stirring, the reek of sewage curling off the slips and coal dust thickening the morning light. A towboat hauling a barge slid past a brig that was tying up, longshoremen already scrambling over her deck. A lone blacksmith's hammer began to clang.

Ellen gripped the iron railing, her fingers white. Wind stirred her hair, and for a fleeting second without her bonnet, she looked like the girl he used to know—the one who was always staring past the horizon, hungry for something more.

The whistle shrieked. A final jolt ran through the deck as the mooring lines snapped taut.

Perk adjusted his hold on her sea chest. His grip was steady, but his stomach twisted when he found himself too laden with baggage to take her arm. That simple shock pierced him. No way to keep her safe. To keep her close.

In minutes she'd be gone.

West Street sprawled along the waterfront, a tangled mess of carts, drays, and half-frozen muck. Already the city was moving toward full steam—with stevedores shouting over the bang and scrape of crates in the netting.

Perk lingered, watching Ellen square her shoulders as if eager to claim her place in the tangle. The moment they stepped down that gangway, everything would change.

The deckhands worked fast, lowering the gangplank with practiced efficiency, but Perk descended it slower than he should have. Slower still when they reached the wooden pier. He stayed close to

Ellen, shoulder pressed against hers, keeping a half step between her and the worst of the slush.

The boards could be slick this time of year, he told himself. Could send her sprawling. A cart rattled past over the cobbles, piled high with crates stamped HAVANA, sending a flock of pigeons skyward in a panic of beating wings.

Too soon, they reached West Street. He glanced at the clock affixed to the ticket office of the New York & Boston Steam Packet Company.

8:42.

The city enveloped them. A pair of boys darted through the street dragging a mongrel by a length of rope. The painted ladies in the doorways were already eyeing Perk, shifting their bright shawls, the scarlet color cutting sharp against the dull, gray light.

It was time to part ways.

THE WEIGHT of it hit him harder than he expected. Not just the inevitability of it, but the finality. The sharp knowledge that, most likely, he'd never see Ellen again.

He fought the tightness in his chest. The slow, slick thud of his own heart. His mortification had dulled to sadness, his anger to fatigue. Both left him unprotected for the sudden, sweet memory of their time as children, deciding that one day they'd explore that horizon line together.

The God line.

In the past ten years, sailing had become a job, he realized, same as any other. A hard one—maybe the hardest. The sea would give him towering graybeards one day and a dead calm the next. A port was a port. Cargo was cargo. Time was money, and speed was king.

But once upon a time—with her—sailing had been a dream. A fantasy, even. The sea had meant freedom. The wind, a promise. And China had been a mysterious, magical place, waiting to be discovered.

For a moment, Perk reveled in the miracle of what he'd had the great fortune to experience—so much larger a life than he'd ever expected.

The five-story pagoda. The forest of junks and sampans where families lived their whole lives on the water, cooking over charcoal braziers and hanging their washing on the rigging. The deep, sonorous gong strikes rolling over the Pearl River. The heady smell of hot pork dumplings, thick in the night air.

The Thirteen Factories, with their British, American, Dutch, and Swedish flags snapping. Whitewashed walls and clerks in neatly pressed suits. The only sliver of land where foreign devils were permitted to trade. And beyond that, the city proper, forbidden and wild—flower boats glowing with candlelight, opium crates unloaded by silent hands, the narrow alleys where he'd secretly walked once, twice, a dozen times, just to see it. Just to know what lay beyond the invisible walls drawn around.

All thanks to a seed Ellen had planted long ago.

The realization gripped him, sharp and sudden, a hook set deep in his gut. The itch to get back to his ship surged like a St. John's tide. Not for the respect. Not for the responsibility or the damned manifests.

For the thrill. For the chase.

For one more chance to win.

He wouldn't miss her trigonometry and statistics lessons, but he'd certainly miss her. Her stubbornness. Her sharp wit. The easy, unthinking laughter. The way he could say things he wouldn't admit to another soul, and the way she'd answer without hesitation, like she knew exactly what he meant.

He adjusted the chest on his shoulder, shifting the weight. New York pressed in around, but for one moment—one breath of space— there was nothing between them but silence.

Despite everything, he'd miss her.

And that was the worst truth of all.

. . .

THE SMELL of grease and frying onions rolled in from a vendor's cart. A boy, no more than ten, stood beside the pan, flipping cornmeal mush in sizzling fat, the crust crisping golden at the edges. Perk's stomach let out a low growl before he could stop it.

He checked the clock—8:52.

The least he could do was buy her breakfast.

He shifted his weight, rolling his shoulders against the ache settling into his back. "Where will you go now?" he asked, fishing out a coin while balancing the chest on his shoulder and basket against his knee.

Ellen barely glanced around. Her focus stayed on some spot near his chest, like she could stare right through him. "I'll take a room," she said.

A man in a bottle-green frock coat passed, flicking his eyes over Ellen—once, twice, taking the full measure of her. Drawn by her bonnet-less hair, no doubt. Perk's fingers curled with the sudden urge to smash his teeth into the cobbles.

Ellen was plenty capable, but the city didn't care about that. Without money, without prospects, she was just another face in the crowd. A mark for pickpockets. A target for any madam looking to recruit fresh girls.

The contents of the chest would be worth enough to keep her fed for months—but all his efforts would be useless if it was stolen by midmorning.

"You know you have to be careful," Perk said, handing over the corn cake and keeping his voice even. "It's a big city and not everyone—"

"I do, Perk." She glared at him, sharp and sudden. "Thank you for your concern." Her voice was tight. "You know I've been here before, though. Many times. Far longer than you've been coming, actually. It's one of the reasons I—"

She stopped. Just like that, her gaze dropped to the street. A wharf rat could've run by.

But Perk certainly couldn't forget the way she used to lord her travels over him when they were young. When he was stuck in a ropewalk ditch, choking on hemp fibers and running miles on end—backward.

You'd love New York City, Perk. You should visit one day. They have omnibuses to take you anywhere and gas lights that turn night into midday.

But that was before. When her father was a schooner captain and Perk's was a disgrace. When she was the girl with all the freedom in the world and he was the boy breaking himself in half to earn a crumb of dignity.

Good God, he was glad those days were gone.

Two MILES across town and he'd be back aboard the *Oneida*. He'd be Captain Creesy. And the past could stay where it belonged.

"Thank you for the navigation lesson," he said, aiming for neutral ground. A clean ending. "We're square with our deal. I wish you—"

The words twisted, caught somewhere between his chest and his throat.

A pleasant life? Good luck pretending to be a man?

None of it sat right.

"I wish you well."

He hesitated, gripping the sea chest, uncertain what to do next. He couldn't set it down—the ground was thick with offal and filth. A pile of rotting vegetables lay half-trodden into the gutter. But he couldn't hand it to her, either. She wasn't Elliot yet. Her hair was still long and wild, and she wore a dress, petticoats, button boots. What kind of man would burden a woman with such baggage?

Soon enough, if she was serious about this mad plan of hers, she'd have to manage her own chest. Her own halyards and reefing lines.

The thought sent another tremor through him. Sailors died on every voyage. Men stronger than her. More experienced than her. All it took was one moment of bad luck. One misstep aloft. A hand in the wrong place when the wind shifted. A wave breaking wrong over the rail. The sea didn't care if you were reckless or careful. If it came for you, that was it.

His chest was pounding.

But she wasn't his responsibility. She'd made that clear enough.

Absolutely not, Captain Creesy.

He hoped she might land herself a berth on a North River barge. Something slow. Closer to safe. Captained by a man with the sense to stay in port when the weather soured.

He checked the clock again—9:02.

HE'D MAKE TIME. A few minutes to walk her across to a boarding house, then he'd run across town. Sprint if he had to.

"Which rooming house do you fancy?" He asked, nodding toward the rows along West Street. "I'll see you that far, at least."

"There's a place I remember," she said. "Near the Tontine Coffee House."

Perk grimaced. That was off South Street. Not where the canal boats and passenger ferries docked. Not where she had a prayer of staying safe. No, her plans—her delusions—were bigger than that. She was aiming all the way across town at the deep-water docks. The coastal traders. The Liverpool packets. The tea ships.

Ships like the *Oneida*.

It was lunacy. But what choice did he have? He'd given his word.

"Come on," Perk said, voice tight, already turning south, realizing the time was slipping through his fingers. If they went two blocks down to Rector, then cut east along Wall Street, they'd come out on South Street at Dock 15, by the coffee house—and the *Oneida*.

It would be tight, and with her and her baggage in tow, he couldn't run to make up for it. It might be after ten by the time he arrived. There'd be no time to check the stowage or make sure Austin hadn't lined his pockets with silver from the chests. Perk would have to trust the manifests.

He'd gone five steps before he realized she wasn't beside him.

. . .

HE TURNED, pulse hammering, to find her still standing where he'd left her, feet planted like roots in the street. That look on her face—stubborn, set—snapped something inside him.

"My ship gets tugged out of her berth at eleven with or without me," he bit out the words, sharp with the pressure building in his chest. "And I've got quite a bit of preparation—"

"—Perk, you're wrong to—"

"It's not up for discussion." His blood was boiling now, hot under his skin. "I'm not leaving you on the street. I'll see you safe in a rooming house, and there'll be no argument about it."

"That's not what—"

"Would you shut up for once?"

The words cracked, louder than he meant, but he didn't care. God knew he'd regret it later, but right now, the weight of his worry manifested in fury. He didn't have time for this. He didn't have patience.

"Just listen for one bloody time in your life, Ellen, and follow me. Now!"

Her hands curled into fists. She planted them on her hips, standing firm.

"I will not."

Perk clenched his jaw so hard that his teeth ached.

Good God, that woman.

He had half a mind to dump her chest right there in the filth and be done with her. Let her sort herself out. But he wouldn't let her win that easy.

"You will."

The words came slow, deliberate, as he forced down the urge to shout. He had no mate to subdue her. Couldn't haul her up by the collar, couldn't threaten to have her flogged into obedience.

"You're wrong."

He let out a short, bitter laugh.

"Wrong? That's rich, coming from you!" People were starting to notice. He could feel their eyes sliding toward them, quick and wary. He didn't care. The anger twisting through him was welcome. It was honest.

"Goddamn it, Ellen! Who do you think you are?" The words came hot, unfiltered, ripped straight from a festering wound. "You and all your lies? Betraying everything you promised and leaving me to take the damn fall? You think you can tell me what's wrong?"

The attic came back to Perk in a rush. The ropes. The torn flesh at his wrists. The stifling heat. The acrid stink of piss in the corner. The sound of Father's boots on the stairs.

"Tossing about ideas of marriage like I was a plaything," he shouted, "Then slamming the door in my face? Toying with the affection you knew I had for you? Crushing me like a bug under your boot and then asking for the favor of an escort—a favor I was fool enough to grant!"

His voice was rough, breaking under the weight of it all.

Stupid, lovesick boy.

Stupid, lovesick man.

He could've driven his fist straight through the nearest brick wall.

"How do you plan to humiliate me next? Keep me from my ship before she sails? Are you in league with my father now, too? What is it, Ellen?"

"Your route."

He'd been waiting for her to fight back. Waiting for her to match his rage with hers, to throw words just as sharp. When she didn't, his fury turned on itself, tangled in confusion.

"You're headed straight for the tea ship docks," she said, calm as if he hadn't just torn himself open in front of her.

He was sinking fast. Not following. Charged up with a fight that had nowhere to go. "Of course I am! That's where we're bloody headed!"

"Yes." She nodded, voice infuriatingly steady. "But you've not calculated correctly. The direct route will be vastly slower than the indirect one, and if you go that way you'll not make it by eleven. You'll miss your ship, Perk."

That rankled. Her condescension. Her treating him like he didn't understand how to get from one side of the city to another.

"Don't you see?" she added. "This is what I've been trying to explain all night. This is how Waterman and Palmer and Howland sail laps around you at sea."

His fists clenched tighter and he nearly did punch the wall.

She pointed across town. "Wall Street is the direct route, but the markets have just opened, so you'll face merchants flooding the walks, jostling to hear stock prices, pushcart vendors jamming the curbs, newsboys running their papers in and out of every doorway, banker's carriages, omnibuses, and delivery wagons in a snarl of contrary currents."

She paused as if to let the picture settle. Let him see it. Then she continued. "If we do manage to fight our way through that mess, as soon as we hit Broadway, we'd get trapped in the construction chaos around Trinity Church and be unable to move. Stuck in the doldrums, the clock would run out and your ship would leave without you."

He stared at her, mouth agape.

"But if we go but a little out of our way first, north to Cedar, we'll have a free path east. Just a few craftsmen and washerwomen out this time of day. And when we do cross Broadway, it won't be at a chokepoint."

Her eyes locked on Perk's. "Are you following?"

The worst part? He was.

"Do you see now? The oceans have streets just like New York," she continued. "You've been picking the most direct route while your rivals have discovered that sometimes the indirect ones can shave weeks off a voyage, like a shortcut through the sea."

He didn't want to believe her. He wanted to cling to his anger, his certainty, his goddamn pride.

But she was right.

"You've spent the past three years at sea trying to muscle your way through Wall Street," she said. "When Cedar was right there all along."

Perk felt it, same as he felt a storm coming in his bones. Her indirect route through the city would get them there significantly faster than his direct one. The shock of it stopped him in his tracks. A gust of wind lifted the collar of his coat, chilling the sweat on the back of his neck. She was right. To survive as a captain, much less win, required both tactics and strategy.

He'd never win a race without her.

SHE WAS INSUFFERABLE. High and mighty as a harbor pilot, treating him like a greenhorn on his first passage.

She was also brilliant.

His ceaseless efforts to wrest every quarter-knot of speed from the *Oneida*—running full sail day and night, re-trimming the yards at every bell, punching through storms rather than running from them— that was only half the battle.

The other half was discovering the invisible bands of water and air, thousands of miles away, that marked those shortcuts.

Ellen's half.

If she'd obey her captain, could he live without her vowing to obey her husband?

"Follow me," she said.

And he did.

13

———

"Is she still there?" Ellen asked, breathless. "Your ship?"

She'd forgotten how dizzying the tumult of South Street could be—until a flour carter nearly crushed her against the bricks of a sailmaker's loft. Judging by the shocking sounds emanating from the upstairs window, it doubled as a sailor's bawdy house.

"Can't tell yet," Perk called back, three steps ahead.

ELLEN PUSHED her way southward through ghostly low clouds, veiling the churning sea of stevedores and draymen, fishwives and crimps, everyone jostling for purchase on the narrow strip of paving blocks. A bitterly cold rain had begun to fall, soaking her through and plastering her bonnet-less hair to her cheek. She was suddenly very grateful Perk had bought her oilskins, though she wished she'd had the foresight to put on the sou'wester before they left the steamer.

Perk, tall and broad, pushed through the current and she was glad to have his strength. She barely sidestepped a pile of manure, tamped down her unease and pressed forward, hugging the buildings against the churning tide of bodies.

Near the corner, a group of angry men shouted down a woman—not a working girl or a beggar, she realized, but a speaker. A woman who'd dared mount a hogshead to make her case about something or other. A woman. Daring to speak in public.

Ellen was dismayed but kept her head down. She'd promised to get Perk to his ship in time, and that was her sole mission. She didn't think it was quite eleven quite yet, but try as she might, she couldn't spot a clock face anywhere.

"Which berth?"

But he was too far ahead to hear her. She followed Perk as he angled into the street, away from the crowds seeking limited shelter on the walk, and suddenly spotted the bowsprits through the mist. Her heart swelled to behold the whole canopy of them, crossing over the street like the flying buttresses of some maritime cathedral.

A few doors down she found the looming façade of Grinnell & Minturn's office. They must be close to his ship. Behind one great arched window a figure moved behind the glass. A clerk, perhaps. Or maybe Grinnell himself, surveying his domain from above.

"Here," Perk circled back, grabbed her hand, and pulled her past a newsboy calling out something about British warships in the Orient, and then around two sailors brawling violently in the street.

They emerged on the slightly less crowded finger of Dock 19, where the last provisioning carts had been emptied and the ratcatchers were out in force.

"Welcome," Perk said, panting. "To the *Oneida*."

Ellen stopped short, fighting for breath after the hustle across town. When she turned to take in the massive, black-painted hull beside her, she gasped in awe. Had the *Oneida* been a building, it would have been one of the largest she'd ever seen. Set on her stern end, she estimated it would have stretched twelve stories high, into the very heavens.

"This? This is *yours*?" The wind whipped the last of her hair from its fastenings as she turned back to Perk. An unfamiliar squint set in his eyes and he gave her the curt nod of a captain in full view of his crew.

"That she is."

The air was frigid but his voice was warm. Inviting, even.

Ellen couldn't have said what she'd expected, but it wasn't this. The *Californian* had seemed so immense, she'd almost forgotten that larger giants existed. But Captain Papa's schooner was 90 tons and Perk had said the *Oneida* was 750. The ratio was easy enough to calculate, yet her imagination had utterly failed to create a vessel more than eight times larger. A ship sailing routes Captain Papa could only have dreamed of. A vast machine of such complexity would take a rare kind of captain to run her.

Her heart swelled with awe—pride, even—as she envisioned Perk on the quarterdeck. No one with salt in her blood could look at a ship like that and not wonder what it would be like to sail her. Ellen would have given her last breath for a tour if he'd not been in such a hurry to leave, for a chance to trace the ship's lines with her own hands.

But the steam tug was already nosing into position, black smoke curling from the stack as a deckhand prepared the heaving line. No time for admiration, and yet Ellen stood rooted, drinking in the sight.

Shadows moved on the main yard, crewmen, still bending on a sail, strapping men but struggling like mad as wind gusts tried to fill the canvas before it was ready. Leaving it a bit late, she thought. Perk'd probably have their guts for garters once he got aboard.

The yard stretched impossibly wide. Ellen judged the *Oneida*'s beam to be around thirty-five feet, making the yards at least seventy feet across. So wide that a shout from one end seemed as if it would go unheard at the other. But they must have communicated somehow because as soon as one man spotted Perk on the dock, in a flash they were all staring at him, grins wide.

No, she realized. Staring at her.

The captain had a lady friend. Well, soon enough their

wondering would come to naught once he left her on the docks, soon to become—what?

A sailor? *A man?*

SHE'D MISJUDGED MORE than the scope of the *Oneida*, Ellen realized with a stab of fear. She was strong for her petite size and plenty determined, but the canvas they bent on the *Oneida*'s main yard was so large it could have swallowed a countinghouse. A dozen men with bodies like oxen were struggling to haul it properly, standing on a thin line, eighty feet above the deck.

Over the past twenty-four hours, she'd convinced herself she could become a sailor, but she'd been lazily imagining a ship more like the *Californian*, that had almost exclusively used fore-and-aft sails—ones that could be set easily from the deck with a small crew without much difficulty.

But there at the dock, her dream dissolved in the rain, as she was vividly reminded that an oceangoing ship like the *Oneida* sailed primarily with its square sails. Ones that took the strongest of men to subdue.

"Ellen."

No sweet, family-run schooners here. This was a world of men, thick with labor and muscle, hands black with tar and sweat.

She'd been around deepwater vessels before. How had she let desperation draw her into such an impossible fantasy? Furious as she was at herself, standing beneath the *Oneida*, she couldn't help but see the reality. If anything, the ships were larger than she remembered. Their decks towering above her like cliffs.

If the point wasn't clear enough, right in front of her a young deckhand got kicked square in the shin by a pig as it was being slung aboard—a blow to nearly shatter a bone—but he swore at the animal and got back to work. At the next dock over, men fought—literally fought—for a spot on a crew. Burly sailors circling each other like dogs.

To reach a navigator's position without a reference or family connection, she'd have to work her way up same as Perk had—starting as crew. Even if she managed to get a position, could she keep it? She tried to envision herself among a crew, trading punches. Could she win a brawl? Survive one, even?

And what if she did manage to become a brawling, canvas-wrestling crewman? Would she be acting as her truest self or would it merely be one more role she was ill-suited for? No different than baking cookies or knitting gloves.

"Ellen."

Perk coughed behind her. Probably trying to cut their departure short so he could scurry up the boarding ladder and be off. She knew she should say goodbye and give him leave, but first she had to clear away any hint of fear in her eyes.

She scanned South Street, desperate to see at least one woman working a job other than on her back. Most of them were either wives or whores—dressed either to attract attention or to avoid it altogether. Of course. It must be dangerous to be mistaken for the wrong one.

There was a stout, red-faced woman hauling a basket of laundry into a rooming house, though. Another selling fish. And there, a woman Ellen's age, balancing a tray of pewter mugs as she wove between the tables of a dockside pub. She guessed most were likely turning tricks on the side to make ends meet. But perhaps, gainful employment for a woman on land wasn't entirely out of the question.

The rain turned to snow, colder but lighter, swirling in the gusts. She squared her shoulders, crushed that she'd never get closer to a full-rigged ship than it's bowsprit, but determined to chart her own course.

As she was working through the possibilities of becoming a barmaid, Perk caught her sleeve. She turned slowly, not ready to hear the word goodbye.

He was looking at her like a man who'd made a decision. Not waiting, not weighing, just steady as the tide.

"Marry me, Ellen," he said.

She inhaled sharply, fighting both fear and desire in the same breath, terrified at how close he was to toppling her resolve.

"We've had this conversation."

"Aye," he said, voice low. "So let's have it again."

Above, the *Oneida*'s crew caught towlines tossed from the tug.

"What if I didn't ask you to obey?"

"Perk—"

It came out as a whisper. All she could manage. Her compass swung wildly in every direction.

Saying the wrong thing once had cost her ten years of friendship. The second time nearly broke them. There would be no third.

The steam tug's whistle shrieked, shrill and impatient, echoing off the buildings. Their time was running out.

Brawling sailors. Red-faced laundress. Speaker pulled from a hogshead.

Where did she belong?

A flicker of vulnerability crossed Perk's eyes, a rawness she hadn't seen since they were children. He took a deep breath, as if steadying himself against a heavy swell.

"As captain and navigator, you'd need to respect my authority same as would any officer I took on. But as man and wife, you've my word that we'd be equals. It's my best offer."

She stared at him, heart flopping like a caught fish. The world had shifted in an instant, fraught with both greater promise and greater danger.

THIS WAS what she had always wanted, wasn't it? A chance to be valued for her mind, her skills, to be herself. There would be freedom, wind in her hair, the horizon—and Perk.

She looked up once again at the *Oneida*. A tall, disapproving figure leaned over the monkey rail on her quarterdeck. Austin, no doubt, eyeing her like a bit of flotsam washed up on the docks.

Was this her salvation or another kind of trap? A 750-ton ocean-going cage with a lifetime commitment?

For that matter, which Perk would she get? The old Perk she recognized like her own heart or the new Perk who'd grown more commanding but also darker?

Someone she loved or someone she didn't know at all?

What were the chances they could make this work?

Despite the prying eyes and sopping wet dock, Perk settled himself down on one knee, placed her sea chest on the other, and lifted the lid.

Even in the flat gray light, the brass gleamed.

Ellen could practically feel the weight of it in her hands, the precise way the mirrors would catch the sky.

He'd bought her the sextant.

Not a cast-off from an old trader, not a battered tool that had lived through storms and careless hands, but the brand-new instrument in Delano's window. For a moment, everything else—the ship, the mate, the pressure, the future—faded to the edges.

The instrument was heavy. It was real. It was hers.

It held the power to pull a star down to the horizon, to bend the vast distances of the universe, to see the invisible and fix the unknowable to guide a ship safely through the darkness.

She could align the very heavens, but had no idea how to do the same with two wild hearts.

The tugboat leaned on its horn again, impatient to get going.

"You'll have to give an answer now, I'm afraid." Perk said, gently sliding one of her hands into his—a gesture of either greeting or parting.

The weather had frozen his fingers near as raw as hers, but with their palms pressed together, Ellen felt a warmth generated that almost seemed to defy the conditions.

"The chest and its contents are yours regardless, but I must either take my leave now or flag down a neighboring captain to perform a short ceremony on deck."

ELLEN TOOK A DEEP BREATH, closed her eyes, and followed Captain Papa's training for how to evaluate varying courses.

Step one: Establish the knowns and unknowns.

I'm thrilled. I'm terrified.

I know him, but I don't.

This is a chance of a lifetime. This is a lifetime commitment.

Step two: Reduce error by investigating any doubts.

I could be a great navigator.

Nothing like this has ever been done before.

Perk is like quicksilver rolling under my skin.

Step three: If resolution remains unclear, pick a heading and sail it until new information demands correction.

I need freedom. I need Perk.

The answer was indivisible.

THE SHIVER HIT HER FIRST. Then the meaning of it. This problem was unlike any she'd ever encountered. No equation, no observation, no careful plotting could reduce it further.

The conflict between her needs would never resolve. The tides of their life together would forever rise and fall, ebb and flow.

It was the impossible square root of two—the problem that had stymied even Pythagoras. The exception that proved that rules weren't universal truths, but ideas, written down by people, and then taken as fact.

And if the great Pythagoras could be wrong, so too could Pastor Bartlett. And Marblehead. And maybe even the seafaring world at large.

The uncertainty of the venture, the risk, the raw impossibility, was also the very core of its beauty. Their course together was indeterminate. As unsolvable as a ship knowing what storms may come weeks after she sets sail.

It might be a dream come true. It might be a never-ending nightmare. Most probably, it would be some combination of both.

Ellen opened her eyes and searched Perk's earnest face, the sextant at his knee, and then the horizon line. Something shifted inside her. That moment a ship catches the wind and surges forward, committed to its journey, no matter what might lie ahead.

On that instinct alone, she made her decision.

Of course you can do this, Eleanor Prentiss.

THE END

―――

IF YOU ENJOYED *THE NAVIGATOR*, you can dive deeper into Ellen and Perk's past with the short story *Salem*. Get your FREE story today at cheyennerichards.com/salem

YOUR REVIEW IS WELCOME

Sharing your honest experience with this book not only helps other people choose books they'll enjoy, it also helps tailor suggestions for you to find your next great read.

———

Speaking of which, read on for a book you won't want to miss.

AFTERWORD

I first heard of Ellen Creesy in 2013, in the middle of my inaugural sailing lesson, when my instructor, Eric Wittig, learned I was a writer and said, "Have I got a story for you."

I was amazed by her feat, then inspired, then intrigued. But I was also trying to control a bucking J24 in twenty-two knots and the heavy chop of San Francisco Bay while being soaked by freezing spray. I filed Ellen away in my mind as a fascinating historical tidbit.

At the time, I was working on a different novel and far more focused on my own relationship with the sea. Was my dream of sailing into the sunset just fantasy, I wondered? Did I even *like* sailing?

That first wild and wet day gave me the answer: an emphatic *YES*!

Over the next several years, I took every class I could, became a skipper, and began chartering boats. Then I joined race teams and learned how to eke every half-knot out of a boat—under pressure, when things were breaking, in the most challenging conditions. Eventually, I was invited to become an instructor myself and discovered that teaching in those same J24s taught me more than I'd ever learned by doing.

Along the way, I fell in love with a fellow sailor who shared my dream. In 2018, we moved aboard a Pacific Seacraft 37 named *Pristine*, set off from San Francisco, and spent the next two years sailing around Baja and into the Sea of Cortez.

I got seasick. I got cold. My sleep was interrupted, my hair was constantly salty, and grocery shopping meant a new market in a new town in a new language every week. There were storms and rocks, sharks and orcas. I rationed water, electricity, and notebook space.

And yet, they were the most glorious years of my life.

Almost daily, nature gave me at least one moment of awe. My coffee cup and pillow stayed in the same place—but every week, my backyard changed completely. Life didn't just include adventure—it *was* adventure. I never wanted the journey to end.

In early 2020, after 5,000 nautical miles, we prepared to cross our first ocean. But three days before departure, Covid closed the Pacific.

What followed was a slow unraveling: we sailed back to California, moved ashore, and ultimately sold the boat. I never stopped dreaming of going back—but for a long while, the only way I could get to sea was through story.

And that's when Ellen resurfaced.

If I couldn't be at sea myself—at least not yet—I could write about it. As I researched her life, I learned she too had lost her dream for a time, when she lost her father. On some level, we were sea sisters. That was enough to dive in headfirst.

Of course, I wondered how she built the skills, courage, and inner strength to succeed. Not just as a person—but as a woman.

One of the most popular preachers of Ellen's day was Edwin Hubbell Chapin, who packed Trinity Church in New York with two thousand congregants each Sunday and inspired the character of Pastor Bartlett. In his *Duties of Young Women* (1849), he wrote:

"It is morally wrong to neglect or violate the laws of our being. The culture of our God-given powers is a religious duty. The display of learning in a woman is disliked as much as pedantry in a man, the strong-minded woman characterized by cold, masculine, intellectuality. The purpose of a woman's intellect is for charming conversation, enriched by judgment, and refined by a discriminating and educated mind."

This was the world Ellen lived in. And yet she didn't just sail— she became the best navigator of her century.

I set out to write about that accomplishment. But I'd been to sea. I'd navigated both a boat—and a marriage—under duress. And I found myself asking a deeper question:

Not just *how* did she do it, but *how did she do it with him?*

Writing *The Navigator* became far more than historical fiction. It became a reckoning. Like many women, I've wrestled with the tension between freedom and belonging, strength and softness, ambition and acceptance. Chapin's words may sound outdated—but poke around on Reddit, where anonymity reveals honesty, and you'll still hear:

"Gender roles have worked since the dawn of time. I have o idea why they want to change it now."

Or ask what men most value in women and you'll find: beauty, loyalty, a family mindset.

We may balk at Chapin's overt rules—but many of his sentiments are still deeply internalized within us.

As a former corporate executive, I've seen the effects firsthand: The men who support strong women—until you outrank them. The staff who label you "difficult" when you speak directly. The subtle pressure to dim your light so others feel more comfortable.

And it's not just women who are trapped.

Ask what women most value in men, and you'll often hear: money, status, and height. The system boxes everyone in.

Ellen's story gave me a language for that struggle—and a vision for transcending it.

It was incredible enough that she became a professional navigator. That she *crushed* it. But she also had to navigate the uncharted waters of being both wife and crew—balancing facts and feelings, strategy and survival, in an environment where mistakes could mean death.

Hers was a sea adventure for the ages. But it was also a marriage story.

This novel is fiction, inspired by real people and events. The heart of it is true, even where the details are imagined.

If you've ever asked yourself whether it's possible to live a life of daring and devotion, of love and liberty—Ellen's journey has an answer. She doesn't offer it neatly wrapped. But it's here, between the lines.

And if this story stirred something in you, keep sailing with us. The voyage of *The Navigator Series* is just beginning.

Cheyenne Richards

May 2025, San Francisco, California

P.S. Just as Ellen went all-in, so did I. While writing this story, my husband and I sold our house and bought a new boat—our future home, and vessel for adventure. We move aboard this November.

The compass is set. The sails are ready. A new chapter awaits us all.

AUTHOR'S NOTES

Eleanor Horton Prentiss Creesy didn't leave much in the historical record to go on, but the accounts of those who interacted with her are almost universally glowing. While sources differ slightly, most indicate that her husband referred to her as Ellen, or occasionally Ellie, which is what I've used in this narrative.

In the same vein, it's reported that Captain Josiah Perkins Creesy commonly went by his middle name, and that—in private, at least—Ellen called him Perk.

As for the surname of Creesy, fixed spelling in the mid-nineteenth century was still a relatively new concept, introduced by dictionaries and public education. You'll find the name spelled any one of twenty-three different ways, including Creesey, Creasy, Creasey, Cresy, Cressy, and Creesie.

New Yorkers may have been surprised to discover that the Hudson River disappeared in this narrative. The early Dutch and English settlers had always referred to it as the North River, and it didn't begin to shift to the Hudson in common usage until the early twentieth century. So I had Ellen and Perk use the terminology that would have been customary in their day.

And sailors familiar with calling the two sides of a ship port and starboard, may have wondered about the term larboard used in this manuscript. The Royal Navy officially began using 'port' in 1844 to reduce confusion, and the US Navy followed in the 1850s. But not only did that occur a few years after the time period of this manuscript, my thinking was that once we learn a system it's a devil to change our habits—however much the change may be for the good. (Just ask an American about adopting the metric system.)

If you'd like to learn more about the real people, ships, and history that inspired this story, here are some of the sources I found especially valuable for researching this novel:

Books and Historical Sources

- *Flying Cloud: The True Story of America's Most Famous Clipper Ship and the Woman Who Guided Her*—David W. Shaw
- *The Flying Cloud and Her First Passengers*—Margaret Elizabeth Lyon and Flora Elizabeth Reynolds
- *Barons of the Sea*—Steven Ujifusa
- *Imperial Twilight: The Opium War and the End of China's Last Golden Age*—Stephen R. Platt
- *Duties of Young Women*—Edwin Hubbell Chapin
- *Some Recollections*—Captain Charles P. Low (commander of the clipper ships *Houqua, Jacob Bell, Samuel Russell,* and *N.B. Palmer*)
- *New York to Boston: Travels in the 1840s*—edited by Robert Hagelstein
- *The Sailor's Word-Book*—Admiral W. H. Smyth
- *Memoir of Robert Bowne Minturn*—Robert Bowne Minturn Jr.
- *A Sea of Words*—Dean King
- *The Wager*—David Grann

- *All Sail Set: A Romance of the Flying Cloud*—Armstrong Sperry
- *Greyhounds of the Sea: The Story of the American Clipper Ship*—Carl C. Cutler
- *The Clipper Ship Era: An Epitome of Famous American and British Clipper Ships, Their Owners, Builders, Commanders, and Crews*—Arthur H. Clark

Museums and Historic Sites

- San Francisco Maritime National Historical Park
- Maritime Museum of San Diego

ACKNOWLEDGMENTS

It takes a village to build a book, and I've been privileged indeed to be surrounded by some of the most generous and talented villagers imaginable.

First, my heartfelt thanks to Eric Witting, who introduced me to Ellen and Perk's story. (True fact: he also introduced me to both sailing and my husband, so I owe this man all the great loves of my life.)

My epic gratitude goes out to the beta readers who helped me turn a pile of pages into a living, breathing story. Thank you Brian Bayley, Suzanne Bayley, Hellern Gregory, Jeni Howland, Kim Ratcliff, Mose Richards, and Mary Starkey. For all the moments you read this novel without feeling confused, bored, or skeptical, you have these brilliant readers to thank.

To my author group, who provided moral support through the messy process of drafting that—for me, at least—seems to always involve one step forward and two chutes back to the start of the game board: Thank you, Wayne R. Key and Sydnee Blodgett, for keeping me going.

To my writer group, who offered critical feedback on both the content and direction of the story: Thank you, Ann Gelder, Gordon Jack, Kim Ratcliff, Matthew S. Rosin, Maricia Scott, and Mary Taugher.

To J. Braun at Mills, who kindly mailed me an out-of-print book that proved invaluable to my research—I'll always remember your generosity to a stranger.

To Laura Duffy, cover designer extraordinaire, for sticking with me through heaps of changes and transitions and creating something stunning and unique. I'm so proud to see it on the front of this book.

To Debra Nichols, the superhuman editor who found and fixed about four zillion instances of author nonsense and grammatical shenanigans.

To the newsletter subscribers who contributed character names for the crew . . . I beg the indulgence of one more book. Your imaginations, research, and ancestors will be honored aboard the ships to come.

And to my husband, Colin Ross, for being my very own Perk—supporting my ambitions, whims, delights, and vulnerable heart through it all. You've endured more museums, dinner-table factoids, and creative insecurities than any one human should be expected to bear, and you've done it with grace and good humor. Thank you, my darling.

Of course, I must also thank the original legends: Eleanor Horton Prentiss Creesy and Captain Josiah Perkins Creesy, for their inspiration. I hope I've captured at least a glimmer of their spirit.

Above all, I offer my deepest appreciation to the most important contributor of all: you, thoughtful reader. Before you picked it up, this book was merely a collection of words. Your imagination provided the alchemy that brought it to life. Thank you for lending this work your beautiful mind.

ABOUT THE AUTHOR

Cheyenne Richards is an award-winning historical fiction author who writes sweeping novels about the women who claimed the sea—drawn from true stories, deep waters, and the lives history nearly forgot. She lives and writes aboard her sailboat *Pristine,* currently working her way around the world. More at cheyennerichards.com.

youtube.com/cheyennerichards

facebook.com/Cheyennerichardswriter

instagram.com/cheyennerichardswriter

ALSO BY CHEYENNE RICHARDS

The Prisoner's Apprentice